Runeterra

League of Legends The VOID

League of Legends, Volume 1

Fandom Books

Published by Fandom Books, 2023.

This is a work of fiction. Similarities to real people, places, or events are entirely coincidental.

LEAGUE OF LEGENDS THE VOID

First edition. June 16, 2023.

Copyright © 2023 Fandom Books.

ISBN: 979-8223847700

Written by Fandom Books.

Table of Contents

- Prologue The Calm Before the Storm 1
- The Harbinger's Message 3
- A Shadow Over Noxus Darius 6
- The Light of Demacia 8
- Piltover's Response 10
- Tensions in Zaun 12
- Voices of the Void 14
- The Glade's Whispers 15
- Unlikely Allies 17
- Zed's Resolution 19
- The Kinkou Order 21
- Unearthed Secrets 23
- Targon's Role 25
- The Calm Before 27
- The Battle Commences 29
- The Tide of War 31
- Hope and Despair 33
- Shurima's Stand 35
- A Twist in the Tale 37
- Rising Again 39
- Alliances Shattered and Formed 41
- The Void Advances 43
- The Battle of Will 45
- Fall of the Titans 47
- A Ray of Hope 49
- The Final Plan 51
- The Great Betrayal 53
- The Last Stand 55
- Victory at a Cost 57
- A New Beginning | - From Ashes to Aspiration 59
- Epilogue | Echoes of a Past, Whispers of a Future 61

A Gathering of Champions	65
Abyssal Tidings	70
Mapping the Unknown	76
The Void's Resistance	80
Unexpected Aid	83
The Echoes of the Past	86
The Frozen Watchers	88
Respite and Revelations	91
Deeper into Darkness	93
The Darkin Blade	97
The Clash of Darkin	99
Void's Heart	101
A Reunion and Revelation	107
Confronting the Voidborn	109
The Void's Origin	111
A Hope in Desolation	115
Victory at a Cost	119
The Aftermath	122
The Homecoming	124
Lessons of the Void	126
The Enigma Unveiled	128
Introduction	131
The Challenge	133
The Selection	135
The First Battle	137
Mystery Unveiled	139
Test of Skill	141
Shadow and Light	143
The Maverick's Gambit	145
The Prize	147
The Second Round	149
The Reveal	151
Showdown of the Shadows	153

A Clash of Chaos and Strategy 155
The Final Duel 157
In the Heat of Battle 159
An Unforeseen Turn 161
A Radiant Victory 162
Secrets of the Prize 163
The Grand Finale 164
Victor's Spoils 166
A New Path 168
The Master Unveiled 170
Aftermath 172
A Strange Disturbance 174
Ripples of Consequences 176

Prologue The Calm Before the Storm

The world of Runeterra, in all its diverse splendor, was a land where magic and mystery intertwined with the fabric of reality, where the supernatural coexisted with the mundane. From the majestic floating cities of Piltover to the golden sands of Shurima, from the icy plains of the Freljord to the towering fortress of Noxus, Runeterra was a world of breathtaking beauty and endless wonders. However, beneath the surface of this tranquil and awe-inspiring world, the seeds of conflict were slowly but surely germinating.

As the sun painted the sky with hues of gold and crimson, Twisted Fate, the Card Master, sat at the bustling port city of Bilgewater, a haven for all kinds of folk – from pirates and smugglers to explorers and thrill-seekers. A myriad of tales echoed within its lively taverns, filling the salty sea air with stories of adventure, danger, and fortune.

While shuffling his deck of mystical cards, Twisted Fate felt an unusual tug at his intuition, a whisper of impending chaos. He drew a card, and its ominous image sent a shiver down his spine – The Harbinger. This was no ordinary hand of fate; it was a prophecy, a forewarning of a calamity that could engulf the entirety of Runeterra.

In Noxus, Darius, the Hand of Noxus, was unaware of the prophecy, yet he sensed a brewing storm. Reports of suspicious activities and whispers of conspiracy had begun to reach his ears. The formidable warrior felt an unease creeping into his heart, a sensation he hadn't experienced in a long while. It was the anticipation of an upcoming battle, and he knew he had to ready his city for the possible onslaught.

Far away in the shining city of Demacia, siblings Garen and Lux Crownguard were grappling with their own concerns. The purity and order of their city seemed under threat, and they found themselves burdened with the responsibility to protect their people and preserve Demacia's ideals.

Simultaneously, in Piltover and its grimy underbelly, Zaun, the enforcers Caitlyn and Vi had their hands full. A city fueled by progress and innovation, Piltover was becoming increasingly vulnerable to its own ambitions, while Zaun was a ticking time bomb of chaos and rebellion.

Meanwhile, in the icy north, Freljord's tribes, led by Ashe and Sejuani, remained oblivious to the world's concerns, embroiled in their own feuds. However, the icy winds seemed to whisper of a greater threat, a threat that could either unite them or shatter their lands.

As these events unfurled across the land, an unsettling darkness began to stir in the depths of the Void, an unfathomable abyss of terror and madness. The prophet Malzahar, tormented by his visions, could only watch helplessly as the dark tentacles of the Void twitched in anticipation of the chaos that was to come.

Thus began the tale of Runeterra, a world teetering on the brink of a colossal conflict. A world where the courage of champions would be tested, alliances would be formed and broken, and the destiny of its inhabitants would hang in the balance. As the dawn of a new day approached, Runeterra held its breath, waiting for the storm that was to come. Little did its people know, they were about to be swept up in a war the likes of which they had never seen before.

The Harbinger's Message

The cheerfulness of the Bilgewater Tavern seemed quite detached from the solitary figure sitting huddled at a corner table. A mess of cobalt blue hair topped a lean, grizzled face focused intently on the deck of cards in his hands. Twisted Fate, as he was known to the locals, was shuffling his deck with an almost obsessive concentration, the colored cards a brilliant blur between his fingers.

The atmosphere changed subtly when a man, his face obscured by a hood, entered the tavern. He moved with purpose, cutting through the drunken revelry until he reached Twisted Fate's secluded spot.

"A message for the Card Master," he muttered, his voice barely rising above the clamor around them.

Twisted Fate paused his shuffling, looking up for the first time to meet the stranger's gaze. He took the proffered parchment without a word, eyes narrowing at the unbroken wax seal. With a quick nod to the messenger who promptly disappeared into the crowd, he turned his attention back to the mysterious parchment.

Breaking the seal with a casual flick of his wrist, he unfurled the paper and began to read. His fingers stilled momentarily, a prophecy of foreboding doom spreading a chill across his heart. It spoke of an approaching calamity, one so vast it could drown Runeterra in shadows.

The cards in his hands seemed to thrum in response, the images dancing before his eyes. He watched, aghast, as one card flipped onto the table of its own accord - The Harbinger. It was a card he knew well, a herald of dire predictions and looming disaster.

Twisted Fate had spent years learning to read the cards, interpreting the arcane symbols to unveil secrets of the future. But the sudden appearance of The Harbinger combined with the ominous prophecy on the parchment left him feeling a chill wind of uncertainty.

Rising from the table, he stashed the cards and prophecy into his coat, pulling it tighter around him. A glance towards the door revealed a night that was deceptively calm, belying the coming storm the prophecy warned of.

With a final look around the now-quiet tavern, Twisted Fate stepped into the chilly night, his thoughts racing ahead. He needed to share this prophecy, needed to gather his allies. The days of friendly games and casual gambles seemed a distant memory. This was a new game, with the highest stakes he'd ever played for.

The image of the Harbinger lingered in his mind as he moved deeper into the shadows. A calamity was coming. It was time for the Card Master to play his hand.

A Shadow Over Noxus Darius

The Hand of Noxus, stood atop the highest tower in the Immortal Bastion, the chilling wind whipping his crimson cloak about him. Below him, Noxus was a sprawling tapestry of stone and iron, a city that reflected the indomitable will of its people.

In the dull twilight, the city looked peaceful, but Darius knew better. Beneath its facade of tranquility, the underbelly of Noxus was rife with deceit and treachery, a battleground as relentless as any he'd fought on. Today, his enemies were not armies but shadows hiding in the city's darkest corners.

His stern features hardened as he turned the information over in his mind. The whisperings, the suspicious movements, the secretive meetings, it all pointed to a coup, a strike at the very heart of Noxus.

As Darius stood against the biting cold, his thoughts were interrupted by a soft, clear voice. "A heavy burden you bear, Hand of Noxus."

Turning around, Darius found himself facing Katarina, the Sinister Blade, her scarlet hair as vibrant as the blood of their foes.

"I trust the evening finds you well, Katarina," he responded, his gaze turning back towards the sprawling city.

"The evening is as it should be, but Noxus...Noxus is not," she said, stepping forward to join him. "Rumors of treachery run as swiftly as the Rampant River."

"I am aware," Darius nodded solemnly, "and I intend to stop it."

Darius's determination was met with a knowing look from Katarina. "A fight within our city walls, it seems we've come full circle."

The Hand of Noxus didn't respond immediately, lost in thoughts of battle plans and tactics. He was a man forged in the crucible of war, and though this was a different kind of battle, he would face it head-on.

"Duty calls us, Katarina. We do what we must for Noxus." His voice was as unwavering as his resolve.

Katarina nodded, her emerald eyes gleaming with the shared resolve. "And so we shall, Darius. For Noxus."

As the night deepened, Darius knew the city he loved was teetering on the brink of a silent war, one that threatened to shatter its foundations. But with his mighty axe in hand and trusted allies by his side, he was ready to defend it, ready to thwart the shadow creeping over Noxus.

The Light of Demacia

Within the serene beauty of Demacia City, bathed in the soft glow of sunset, stood a grand citadel, its gleaming spires reaching for the heavens. Within its walls, Garen Crownguard, the Might of Demacia, stood in the grand library, his eyes tracing over scrolls and maps sprawled across the table.

Footsteps echoed in the chamber, and Lux, the Lady of Luminosity, entered, her golden hair catching the last rays of the day. Seeing her brother hunched over documents, she approached with a gentle smile.

"Garen," she called, her voice a melodious note amid the heavy silence.

Startled, Garen looked up. "Lux," he greeted, his face softening, "You should be resting."

"And let you bear all this burden alone?" Lux responded, moving to stand beside him, her gaze following his to the documents on the table.

"They speak of dark times ahead," Garen said, his voice thick with worry. He pointed to a map of Runeterra, dark lines crisscrossing it. "We may need to prepare Demacia for a fight."

Lux studied the map before turning her gaze to her elder brother, her eyes shimmering with steely determination. "Then we shall rally our forces, Garen. We won't let Demacia fall."

Garen offered her a weary smile, grateful for her unwavering resolve. Their roles may be different - him, the stalwart soldier and her, the beacon of light - but they were united in their love for Demacia.

"There's no one I'd rather have by my side," he confessed, putting a comforting arm around her shoulder. "With you and our people, we can face any storm."

Lux returned his smile, her hand covering his in a silent promise of solidarity. "Together, we can illuminate even the darkest path, Garen."

They stood there for a moment, two pillars of Demacia, their hearts burning with the same fervor. They knew the road ahead would be fraught with peril, but together, they were ready to face it, to protect their home, their Demacia.

Outside, the sun had set, but the radiance of Demacia's hope remained, brighter than ever. The Crownguards were ready, and with them, Demacia would stand firm, even in the face of looming calamity.

Piltover's Response

The city of Piltover, perched high above the cliffs over the district of Zaun, sparkled with the myriad of lights from its towering, brass buildings. A city of progress, where the hum of hextech innovation echoed through its clean, cobbled streets.

The headquarters of Piltover's Wardens, the city's peacekeepers, was a hub of activity, bustling with enforcers. Among them were two notable figures - Caitlyn, the Sheriff of Piltover, and Vi, the Piltover Enforcer, renowned for her gigantic hextech gauntlets.

Caitlyn's office was a maze of crime reports, wanted posters, and maps. At the heart of it all, Caitlyn stood, her eyes narrowed as she studied a dispatch, the severity of its contents furrowing her brow.

Vi entered the office, her heavy boots echoing against the hardwood floor. Seeing Caitlyn's somber expression, she cleared her throat. "What's the word, cupcake?" Vi inquired, leaning against a bookshelf.

"From Twisted Fate," Caitlyn answered, her accent crisp as she handed Vi the dispatch. "He speaks of a looming threat to Runeterra."

Vi skimmed through the dispatch, her frown deepening. "That's bad, real bad. What's our move?"

"We prepare," Caitlyn said simply. Her gaze was steady, the glint in her eyes determined. "We'll reinforce our defenses, patrol our borders, and ensure our hextech arsenal is ready."

Vi straightened, her expression serious. Despite her brash demeanor, she knew when to face things head-on. "Then let's get to it," she replied, clenching her hextech fists.

The two women got to work, their dedication echoing through the bustling headquarters. The city of Piltover, with its brilliant minds and unyielding spirit, would stand against any threat. The city's response, under the leadership of Caitlyn and Vi, was swift and resolute.

Throughout the night, Piltover hummed with a new purpose. Amid the uncertainty, the city's people worked tirelessly, their hopes ignited by the unwavering commitment of their enforcers.

Underneath the starlit sky, Piltover stood tall, a beacon of resilience and unity. Though the threat loomed large, Caitlyn and Vi would do whatever it took to protect their city, to ensure that Piltover remained the city of progress, undeterred by the shadow of conflict.

Tensions in Zaun

Beneath the splendor of Piltover, in the underbelly of the city, lay Zaun, the Undercity. Its dark, smog-filled alleyways a stark contrast to the gleaming towers above. Steam billowed from its haphazardly built factories, and the haunting glow of chem-punk technology illuminated its cobbled streets.

Among the labyrinthine alleys, a raucous commotion echoed, its epicenter a graffiti-splashed square. Jinx, the Loose Cannon, was known for her chaotic antics, and tonight was no different. Fireworks exploded in the night sky, their vibrant colors illuminating the square, where Jinx, with a wild grin, was having the time of her life.

On the fringe of the crowd, Ekko, the Boy Who Shattered Time, watched with a mixture of amusement and concern. He knew Jinx's antics were a spectacle, but tonight, they seemed irresponsible, even dangerous.

"Jinx!" Ekko yelled over the clamor, attempting to make his way through the throng of spectators. "You need to stop this! We've got bigger problems!"

Jinx merely laughed, her eyes sparkling with reckless delight as she lit another firework. "Lighten up, Ekko! It's just a little fun!"

"Fun?" Ekko was incredulous. "You heard about the threat to Runeterra, right? We need to be ready!"

"Oh, so Mr. Time Traveler is scared of a little danger now?" Jinx scoffed, her tone dismissive.

"I'm not scared," Ekko retorted, his gaze intense. "I'm responsible. Zaun is our home, Jinx. We need to protect it."

Their heated exchange ignited a debate within the crowd. Some supported Ekko's call for caution and preparation, while others sided with Jinx, arguing for the need to enjoy the moment, regardless of the impending danger.

As the square erupted in heated discussions, Ekko and Jinx locked gazes. Both were steadfast, each believing in their own approach to the looming conflict. The tension in Zaun thickened, the city's response to the threat becoming as unpredictable as Jinx's next antic.

Voices of the Void

In the vast, barren landscapes of the Shuriman desert, amidst the ruins of a forgotten civilization, stood Prophet Malzahar. His eyes, normally glinting with an uncanny purple light, were now shut tight as he stood in deep concentration. Wrapped in his otherworldly robe, he seemed more a phantom than a man against the shifting dunes.

The desert was silent save for the soft whisper of the wind carrying sand grains in its embrace. Malzahar, however, heard something more, something ordinary ears could not perceive – voices, echoes from the darkest corners of existence, from the Void itself.

"Speak," he implored the wind, his voice barely above a whisper.

Suddenly, his body convulsed as if struck by an unseen force, and his eyes flashed open, revealing the eerie voidlight within. Visions surged into his mind like a flood, images of a world swallowed by darkness, of creatures too alien and horrifying for a sane mind to comprehend. The Void was coming.

"No," Malzahar muttered, sinking to his knees under the weight of his visions. "It's too soon."

For a moment, he tried to reject the prophecy, but the voices were insistent, their whispers turning into a cacophony that echoed in the depths of his being. There was no denying the truth. A cataclysm was on the horizon.

Rising, Malzahar dusted off the sand from his robe. His heart was heavy, but his resolve was unbroken. He knew what he had to do. He would travel across Runeterra, warn its inhabitants, no matter if they scorned him or feared him. He had no choice.

As the desert wind howled, picking up in intensity, Prophet Malzahar set off towards civilization. He carried not just the burden of his visions, but the fate of Runeterra on his shoulders. The Voices of the Void had spoken, and he had listened. Now, it was time for others to hear their harrowing message.

The Glade's Whispers

Nestled amidst the tangled trees of the forest, far from the hustle and bustle of cities and the strife of politics, was the Glade – a magical realm brimming with enchantment, whimsy, and charm. It was home to Lulu, the Fae Sorceress, and Ivern, the Green Father, two champions who embodied the essence of nature and magic.

The Glade was awash with vivid colours, the hues of blossoming flowers, iridescent butterflies, and the ever-changing leaves of mystical trees. A gentle symphony of rustling leaves, chattering critters, and babbling brooks filled the air, enchanting the senses.

On this particular day, however, the Glade seemed unusually quiet, and the air was heavy with a tinge of unease. Lulu, her vibrant purple hair bobbing as she floated in the air, could feel it. Her companion, Pix, a fae spirit, flitted around her anxiously.

"Something's not right, Pix," Lulu said, her brow furrowing as she focused her senses. "Can you feel it?"

Pix chirped in agreement, its tiny form aglow with a faint, worried light.

At that moment, the towering figure of Ivern emerged from a thicket, the vegetation parting to let him pass. He was a being of peace, friend to every creature in the Glade. His features were etched with concern as he joined Lulu.

"The Glade is troubled," he affirmed in his deep, soothing voice. "I hear its whispers on the wind. There's a threat approaching, Lulu, one we cannot ignore."

Lulu nodded, determination replacing worry in her sparkling eyes. "We won't let harm come to our home, Ivern. The Glade has nurtured us, and we will protect it."

Over the next hours, they gathered their powers, calling upon the ancient, untamed magic of the Glade. Wisps of vibrant energy swirled around them, intertwining with the rustling leaves, the running brooks, and the soft glow of the forest. They worked in harmony, strengthening the Glade's defenses, preparing it for the uncertain future that awaited them.

For amidst the cacophony of Runeterra, within the whispers of the Glade, they heard a single, chilling prophecy – the Void was coming. And they would be ready.

Unlikely Allies

The Freljord was a land of eternal winter, where biting winds howled through vast tundra, and snow-capped mountains pierced the skyline. Its people were as resilient and robust as the land they called home - a myriad of tribes each possessing their unique customs and traditions, yet bound together by the ice in their veins and the unyielding harshness of their environment.

Two of these tribes were led by the mighty Ashe, the Frost Archer, and the formidable Sejuani, the Winter's Wrath. Their relationship, much like the terrain of the Freljord, was cold and rife with bitter rivalries. However, as the news of the impending invasion reached the frost-coated plains, they realized they faced a threat that no tribe could tackle alone.

A makeshift council was called, where the two leaders, flanked by their most trusted warriors, gathered in a cavernous hall, aglow with the firelight of burning braziers. The cavern's icy walls echoed with the murmurs of uneasy anticipation as Ashe and Sejuani stepped into the circle of light.

"We may not agree on many things, Sejuani," Ashe began, her voice clear and resolute, "but we can't deny that this threat is bigger than our differences. It's about the survival of Freljord and all its people."

Sejuani, her brow furrowed beneath her helm, met Ashe's gaze. "We've survived before," she replied gruffly, her tone betraying a hint of challenge.

"True, we've weathered storms and endured wars," Ashe retorted, unflinching, "but never against a force such as this. We need to stand together, now more than ever."

The cavern fell silent as Sejuani considered Ashe's words. The idea of an alliance was foreign, even unthinkable, but so was the idea of the Void consuming their homeland. Sejuani finally nodded, a grudging acceptance. "For the Freljord," she said, her voice echoing in the cavern.

"And for our people," Ashe added, nodding back. And so, amidst the frost and the fire, an unlikely alliance was forged – a beacon of hope against the impending darkness.

Zed's Resolution

The Temple of Shadows, lain within the heart of Ionia, was a place where light and darkness coexisted. Its dark stone walls, etched with ancient Ionian inscriptions, flickered in the soft glow of lit candles. Zed, the Master of Shadows, stood solemnly in the main hall, his crimson eyes fixed on the shadowy emblem that adorned the temple's high arch.

His Order, a band of skilled ninjas, trained in the art of shadow magic, gathered before him, awaiting their master's command. They were silent, shrouded figures against the temple's dimly lit backdrop, their faces masked, save for their eyes, glinting with anticipation and respect for the figure that stood before them.

"Brothers and sisters of the Order," Zed began, his voice resonating through the hall, "we are on the precipice of a war that will determine the fate of our world."

As Zed spoke, the shadows around him seemed to dance and shimmer, as if reacting to the gravity of his words. He continued, "We may not share the principles of balance that other Ionian orders hold dear, but we share the love for our homeland, and we will fight to protect it."

A hushed murmur ran through the crowd. They were warriors of the shadows, often at odds with other Ionian sects, yet the threat they faced now was indiscriminate, a danger to them all.

"There will be sacrifices," Zed continued, his eyes briefly closing, as if in pain, "but remember - we are shadows. We are unseen, unheard, yet we are vital. We will strike when they least expect, be where they think we are not. We are the unseen protectors of Ionia."

A powerful silence swept over the room as the reality of Zed's words sank in. The shadows around them seemed to grow darker, heavier, a symbol of the daunting task that lay ahead. The members of the Order of Shadow, in this moment, felt more united than ever

- a formidable force ready to combat the impending storm. Zed, their Master, stood steadfast and resolved, a beacon in their sea of darkness.

The Kinkou Order

The Kinkou Monastery, located among the tranquillity of Ionia's rolling hills and whispering streams, stood in stark contrast to the chaos looming over Runeterra. Inside the ornate structure, a trio of figures, each embodying one of the Kinkou Order's guiding principles, convened in the hallowed hall of balance.

Shen, the Eye of Twilight, Akali, the Rogue Assassin, and Kennen, the Heart of the Tempest, sat around a circular table carved from the oldest tree in Ionia. The room was bathed in soft moonlight filtering through the paper lanterns hung from the ornately carved ceiling, casting long, wavering shadows that danced across the room.

Shen, in his traditional blue and silver armour, started the discussion. "The balance of our world is threatened," he said, his deep voice echoing throughout the room. "The Kinkou has always strived to preserve this balance. The impending conflict tests our resolve."

Akali, the youngest amongst them, responded, her emerald eyes showing a flash of defiance. "We have always acted when Ionia needed us. Why should this time be any different?" Her voice was firm, her will unbending.

Kennen, the yordle who seemed eternally youthful, nodded, a flash of lightning briefly illuminating his small figure. "Akali is right. But this is not just about Ionia anymore. This is about all of Runeterra."

Shen's gaze met Kennen's, a silent understanding passing between them. Then he turned to Akali, acknowledging her statement. "You are both right. The Kinkou Order has a duty to Ionia, and to all of Runeterra. We shall intervene, but with caution. The balance must be upheld."

They spent the remaining hours planning their approach, their strategies, their ways of influencing the situation to restore the equilibrium. The Kinkou Order, the preserver of balance, was ready to step into the fray, their determination mirroring the serene, unyielding strength of the Ionia they called home.

Unearthed Secrets

Ryze, the Rune Mage, was no stranger to the world's dangerous corners, having travelled extensively in his mission to gather the World Runes. His current location was a remote, weather-beaten ruin, half swallowed by the endless desert of Shurima, the ancient edifices holding secrets of a time when the world was still young.

Inside the heart of the ruin, he stood before a giant stone wall, tracing the glowing lines of the ancient Runes with his gnarled fingers. His bright blue eyes flickered with an arcane energy that echoed the Runes' radiant glow, casting fantastical shadows across the room. The deep creases on his aged face were a map of countless years spent in relentless pursuit of these dangerous artifacts.

"These Runes are potent," Ryze mumbled to himself, his voice echoing eerily in the vast chamber. "Their power could be a boon or a curse. We must ensure they do not fall into the wrong hands."

With a deft flick of his staff, a scroll unfurled in front of him, revealing countless more Runes, a testament to his lifelong journey. With practiced ease, he started the arduous process of absorbing the Rune's essence into his scroll, a task demanding intense concentration, lest the Rune's untamed energy run wild.

Outside the ruin, the harsh desert wind howled, and a distant sandstorm was slowly creeping its way towards him. However, inside the ruin, Ryze remained undeterred, engrossed in his task. Time seemed to stand still as the Rune slowly dimmed, its power being carefully transferred into his magical scroll.

Exhausted, Ryze finally leaned on his staff, the task completed. The room plunged into darkness, the last vestiges of the Rune's glow fading into oblivion. He gazed upon the scroll, now bearing the imprint of the new Rune. A glimmer of hope, a powerful tool in maintaining the balance in the impending conflict.

"But this must remain a secret," Ryze mused, rolling the scroll back. "Its power, if misused, could bring untold destruction."

With the Rune safely stored, Ryze left the ruins, merging back into the vast Shurima desert, a lone figure against the encroaching sandstorm. His journey was far from over. The secrets he had just unearthed would soon play a pivotal role in the struggle for Runeterra, a fact only he was privy to.

Targon's Role

High atop the peaks of Mount Targon, where the air thinned and the celestial bodies felt close enough to touch, the Solari temple was bathed in the golden glow of the afternoon sun. The usually serene, isolated place was buzzing with an unusual energy. Within the heart of the temple, Leona, the Radiant Dawn, stood resolute. She was a figure of strength, her armour reflecting the sunlight and making her almost as radiant as the celestial body she worshipped.

Across from her, under the shadow of the towering pillars, stood Diana, the scorned Lunari who had returned from exile. She was the moon's chosen, a living testament to the Lunari's power and resilience. Her silvery armor glowed softly in contrast to the harsh light, a visual reminder of the age-old feud between their people.

"War is coming to Runeterra, Diana. We cannot deny this," Leona began, her tone as firm as the mountain they stood on. "The Solari are ready to join the fight. We must use the sun's power to vanquish this darkness."

Diana, her silvery hair shining under the temple's shadow, retorted, "The Lunari have always believed in balance, Leona. Day and night, sun and moon, light and dark. You propose we wage war, but that could disrupt the very balance we swore to protect."

The temple echoed with the silence of their unresolved conflict. Sunlight filtered through the tall windows, casting long, alternating shadows and beams of light across the stone floor, a reflection of their duality.

Leona clenched her jaw, staring at Diana with her unwavering gaze. "We cannot afford to stand by, Diana. If we don't act, there may not be a world left to protect."

Diana met her gaze, her eyes shimmering with an internal light. "There may be another way, Leona. There is wisdom in our teachings, a solution that doesn't involve rushing headfirst into war. We must consult the heavens, seek guidance from the celestial bodies."

Their words hung in the air, both of them unyielding in their stances. Despite their shared history, they were as different as the celestial bodies they worshipped. The Radiant Dawn and the Scorn of the Moon, two aspects of Targon, two sides of the same coin, both striving for the same thing, yet their paths were vastly different.

Finally, Leona sighed, the weight of the world seemingly on her shoulders. "Very well, Diana. We shall seek guidance. But if the heavens remain silent, we must be prepared to fight."

Their meeting concluded, both women looked out of the temple's high window, gazing at the vast world below, each lost in their thoughts, each hoping for a different outcome in the impending conflict.

The Calm Before

All across Runeterra, from the grand city of Demacia to the depths of the ocean surrounding Bilgewater, there was a silence, a stillness that was unsettling in its unnatural calm. This wasn't the comforting quiet of peace, but the anxious hush that fell over the world before the onslaught of a storm.

In Demacia, the illustrious city of justice and honor, Garen stood atop the city walls, overlooking the lands that stretched out as far as the eye could see. His usually stern face bore an expression of quiet contemplation. His heart was heavy with responsibility; his kingdom was on the brink of a war that threatened to engulf all of Runeterra. He turned, his cape swirling around him, and marched back towards the city, his armour clinking in the silence.

Within the muddled alleys and tall, mechanical towers of Piltover, Vi and Caitlyn prepared their defenses. The city was a bastion of progress and invention, and they were determined to protect it. They stood, surveying the cityscape filled with shimmering lights and bustling life, knowing they might soon be plunged into chaos.

Deep in the underbelly of Zaun, Ekko stood amongst the rubble of a forgotten building. His timepiece, a device of his own creation, hummed in his hand. He closed his eyes, feeling the raw energy pulse through him. Despite the danger that lurked over them, Ekko was resolute. He had fought for Zaun before, and he would do it again. The familiar, comforting hum of his timepiece was a constant reminder of what was at stake.

In the peak of Mount Targon, Diana and Leona had set aside their differences, if only temporarily. Both represented two halves of a powerful force and together, they hoped to steer the course of the coming conflict. Their voices echoed in the silent peaks as they prayed to the celestial bodies, hoping for an answer, a sign.

Far away, in the monastic temple of Ionia, Master Yi meditated. His spirit floated on the river of tranquillity, reaching out to sense the balance of the world. Even in his isolated state, he could feel the disturbance, a pulsating energy that disrupted the harmony of the world. He emerged from his meditation, a determination etched on his face.

Everywhere, the factions prepared, each in their own way. There was a quiet determination, a gritted-teeth resolve that bound them all. As the sun dipped below the horizon, a shroud of darkness cloaked Runeterra. The calm before the storm had begun, a silent preamble to the war that was about to be waged. But even in the overwhelming quiet, there was a sense of unity, a shared purpose that echoed in every heart - they would fight, for Runeterra and for their survival.

The Battle Commences

The hush that had descended on Runeterra was suddenly shattered as the first cries of war pierced the silence. From the craggy hills of Noxus to the mystical forest of Ionia, battle cries reverberated through the air, a haunting symphony of chaos and destruction.

In Noxus, Darius, the Hand of Noxus, stood at the helm of his vast army, his crimson axe glinting menacingly in the sunlight. "Noxians," he bellowed, his voice echoing over the silence, "Today, we fight not just for Noxus, but for Runeterra!" His words were met with a deafening roar, a wave of sound that rippled through the army and filled the air with a fierce energy.

In Demacia, Garen led the charge, his sword held high as he rallied his troops. "For Demacia!" he cried out, and like a wave crashing against a cliff, his soldiers rushed forward, their footsteps a thunderous rhythm in the battlefield.

Meanwhile, on the high seas of Bilgewater, Miss Fortune steered her ship into the thick of the battle. Her dual pistols were a blur of motion as she cut through enemy lines, her crimson hair whipping around her like a cloak of fire. "Let's show them what Bilgewater is made of!" she shouted, her words drowned out by the cannon fire and the crashing waves.

On the fringes of the war, where the wild magic of the Glade touched the mortal lands, Lulu and Ivern danced through the battleground. They weaved intricate spells that bloomed into protective enchantments, their magic a colourful spectacle amidst the stark brutality of the battle.

In Piltover, the high-tech city was a fortress, with Caitlyn and Vi coordinating their forces. The city was alive with activity; turrets were being manned, hex-tech weapons prepared. Vi's mechanical fists crushed any opposition, and Caitlyn's precise shots picked off enemies with deadly accuracy. "Keep them at bay!" Caitlyn commanded, her voice calm and collected amidst the chaos.

Down in Zaun, the undercity was a flurry of movement. Ekko zipped through the skirmishes, his timepiece allowing him to be in multiple places at once. "We won't let them trample over Zaun!" he shouted, his voice echoing off the metallic walls.

As the battles unfolded, the reality of the war became evident. The world of Runeterra was a stage, and its factions, the players. The curtain had risen, and the play of power, betrayal, and survival had commenced. And as the sun set, painting the sky in hues of red and orange, the first day of the war came to a brutal end, leaving behind the promise of many more to come.

The Tide of War

The days following the commencement of the war seemed to blur into a continuous cycle of attack and counterattack. The idyllic peace that had once shrouded Runeterra was shattered, replaced with the grim symphony of clashing steel and the heart-rending cries of fallen warriors. Each faction, in their own right, was a force to be reckoned with, and each day the tide of war ebbed and flowed with their fortunes.

In the expansive valleys of Demacia, the Demacians rallied under the unwavering leadership of Garen and Lux. Their soldiers fought with a righteous fervor, their blows striking as a lion defending its pride. "Hold the line, for Demacia!" Garen would yell, his voice cutting through the cacophony of battle. Yet, for every enemy they felled, it seemed two more would rise to take its place.

Conversely, the barren landscape of Noxus told a different tale. Darius, with his indomitable will, led his troops into battle with brutal efficiency. Noxus' strength lay not in defense but offense, and they cut through the enemy lines like a hot blade through butter. Yet, they were not invincible, and as their enemies regrouped and retaliated, Noxus found itself steadily pushed back.

On the golden sands of Shurima, Azir and his Sun Disc held a formidable defense. The vast deserts provided a natural barrier against invaders, and those who dared to step foot on the sun-scorched sands were met with relentless fury. However, even Shurima, with all its ancient power, couldn't hold the line indefinitely.

Bilgewater, known for its lawlessness, surprisingly found order in chaos. Miss Fortune's commanding presence, coupled with the deadly precision of her crew, proved to be a potent force. Their defenses were as unpredictable as the sea they hailed from, and many enemies found themselves meeting a watery grave.

Piltover and Zaun, the city of progress and the undercity, were locked in their battles. Their technology, a spectacle of human innovation, proved to be a game-changer. Yet, amidst their victories, they suffered devastating losses that threatened to shake their resolve.

Meanwhile, within the mystical forest of Ionia, the Kinkou Order, led by Shen, Akali, and Kennen, fought a shadow war. Their quiet, precise strikes countered the enemy's brute force, maintaining a delicate balance.

As the war waged on, the balance of power kept shifting. Victories were won, and defeats were suffered, each turning the tide in favor of one faction or the other. The war had truly begun, and as each day passed, the world of Runeterra was irrevocably changed.

Hope and Despair

The war raged on, a relentless tempest that swept across Runeterra, sparing no realm from its fury. As days turned into weeks, the initial bravado that had spurred the factions forward had dimmed, replaced by a stark realization - the war was far from over. This realization cast long, despairing shadows over the soldiers, yet in those shadows, flickers of hope still stubbornly persisted.

In the towering halls of Noxus, Darius stood at the head of the high table, his scarred face set in grim determination. "We've faced setbacks, yes," he acknowledged, his voice echoing off the stone walls. "But we are Noxians! We do not cower in the face of adversity. We rise!" A cheer rose from the gathered soldiers, a beacon of hope reignited.

Demacia, though bearing its own scars, clung onto hope like a shield. Garen, clad in his gleaming armor, stood before his troops, his gaze steely. Beside him, Lux's staff radiated a soft, comforting light. "Look around you," he urged, his voice resonating across the silence. "Look at your brothers and sisters, standing tall, unbowed. We are Demacians. We stand together. And together, we will prevail!"

In the depths of the undercity of Zaun, despair seemed to cling to the grimy walls. Yet, amidst the desperation, a spark of rebellion, a refusal to surrender, kept them going. Ekko, with Jinx at his side, rallied the denizens of Zaun. "We've been through worse," Ekko reminded them, his voice steady, his eyes alight with defiance. "We didn't back down then, and we won't back down now."

Within the serene forests of Ionia, the members of the Kinkou Order gathered, their faces masked but their apprehension palpable. Shen, his stance calm and controlled, addressed them. "The shadows of despair may surround us, but we must not let them overcome us. We are the Kinkou, keepers of harmony. Let our purpose guide us through these troubled times."

In the rough and unpredictable seas of Bilgewater, Miss Fortune stood on the bow of her ship, facing her crew. "We've navigated storms before, and we've always found our way," she shouted over the howling winds. "This war is just another storm. We will survive. We will thrive!"

Through hope and despair, the factions persevered, their resolve hardened by the trials of war. Each victory brought a surge of hope, each defeat a cloud of despair. But through it all, they pressed on, for they knew that surrender was not an option. Not when so much was at stake.

Shurima's Stand

Shurima, a land born anew, arose from its slumber like a phoenix from the ashes, bathed in golden light and shimmering sands. At its heart stood Azir, the Emperor of Sands, a regal figure glistening beneath the relentless desert sun. He knew the burden of his role, the responsibility to his resurrected city and its people. He also knew that this conflict, tearing across Runeterra, would not spare Shurima. It was time for them to make their stand.

The sun was nearing its zenith when Azir made his way to the Sun Disc, the monumental edifice that stood as a testament to Shurima's glory. He moved with a royal grace, each step imprinting on the sand, leaving a trail of authority in his wake. He was no stranger to war, but this time, he had more than just his legacy to protect.

As he stepped into the radiant light beneath the Disc, a murmur ran through the crowd that had gathered. There were men, women, children, all looking up to him, their expressions filled with anticipation, worry, and determination. They were Shurimans, his people, and he would lead them, not to their doom, but to their destiny.

He raised his arms, a symbol of reassurance, and began to speak. His voice, strong and sure, carried clearly across the gathering. "Shurimans," he said, "The sands of time have shifted. War is upon us, a war that threatens to consume not just Shurima, but all of Runeterra."

He paused, his gaze sweeping across the crowd. "I won't lie to you," he continued. "The days ahead will be filled with hardship and peril. But remember, we are the children of the sun. We are the heirs of an empire that once stood unchallenged. We will not falter. We will not fail."

A chorus of agreement rippled through the crowd. Azir nodded, a spark of pride flickering in his eyes. "We will stand together, like the pillars of this great city. We will hold the line against whatever comes. We are Shurimans. We do not bow to the storm; we weather it. We are not the grains of sand to be swept away by the wind; we are the dunes that stand tall and resolute."

As he spoke, his words carried the weight of history, the power of an empire reborn. His voice echoed across the vast expanses of Shurima, resonating with the clattering of weapons being readied and the thumping of resolute hearts. They were not simply preparing for a war; they were preparing to stand their ground, to protect their home and their future.

Azir looked at his people, their faces resolute and unyielding. "Stand with me, Shurimans. Stand for our home, our legacy. Stand for Shurima!"

And as one, they roared in response, their voices echoing off the golden structures, filling the air with the sound of undying resolve. They were ready to face whatever came their way. They were Shurima's last stand.

A Twist in the Tale

The frigid winds of Freljord howled, scattering flurries of snow across the frost-riddled landscape. The city of Rakelstake, a testament to the fortitude of the Winter's Claw tribe, bustled with an atmosphere of frenzied preparation. The snow-crusted, solid wooden structures echoed with the rhythm of hammers and axes. The proud warriors of the north, led by the indomitable Sejuani, had allied themselves with Ashe and the Avarosan tribe in the face of impending doom.

In the heart of the city, within the imposing council hall, a meeting of the utmost importance was taking place. The leaders of Freljord's disparate tribes had convened, each voicing their stance on their combined war strategy. Ashe, the Frost Archer, known for her diplomacy, and Sejuani, the Fury of the North, admired for her sheer strength, were leading the discussion.

"We must fortify our defenses and brace ourselves for their attack," Ashe was saying, her fingers tracing the rough contours of a carved wooden map spread across the table. Her pale blue eyes bore an intensity that contrasted her usually calm demeanor. She looked up, meeting the eyes of the other tribe leaders, finally resting on Sejuani.

Sejuani, astride her imposing tusked mount, Bristle, was a formidable figure. Her gaze was icy, her jaw set, her grip on her flail firm. "No, Ashe," she responded, her voice ringing out in the hall, "we won't win this by cowering behind walls. We strike first, we strike hard."

The tension in the room was palpable. A subtle shift in alliances, a slight change in demeanor could tip the scale of balance in Freljord. And just as the tension reached its peak, the unthinkable happened.

Lissandra, the Ice Witch, known for her ancient wisdom and mysterious aura, stood up. Her eyes, a chilling azure, glinted with an unreadable emotion. "I think," she began, her voice a whisper that seemed to command silence, "I think Sejuani is right. We strike."

The silence that followed was deafening. All eyes turned to Lissandra, the gravity of her words sinking in. Ashe looked at her, a mix of disbelief and betrayal in her eyes. The Avarosans had always considered the Frostguard allies. This, coming from Lissandra, was a blow they hadn't anticipated.

A murmur ran through the room, escalating into loud debates. The fragile alliance was teetering on the brink of collapse. The noise was deafening, the confusion was rampant, but amidst all of it, Lissandra stood silent and unmoving, a sinister smirk playing on her lips. The game had changed, alliances had shifted, and the war was about to take a very different turn.

Rising Again

In the glimmering heart of the Avarosan tribe's territory, a feeling of shock and betrayal still hung in the air like a bitter, icy mist. Rakelstake, once a site of united purpose, was now a city in turmoil. The delicate alliance, crafted with so much care and patience, had been shattered. Yet, amidst the confusion and anger, a spark of determination was ignited.

Ashe, the Frost Archer, stood on the snow-covered parapet of the city walls, her gaze sweeping over the sprawl of her tribe's territory. The air around her was chill, but her heart was aflame with resolve. Betrayal had a way of leaving deep wounds, but it also had a way of fostering resolve. She turned to face her council, her icy eyes shimmering with a firm resolve.

"We have been deceived, true," she said, her voice steady despite the betrayal that still stung, "But we will not let this define us. We will rise. We are the Avarosans; we do not back down."

The warriors around her, hardened men and women who had faced the brutalities of Freljord, nodded. Their loyalty to Ashe was unwavering. She was their leader, their guiding star. Her strength in the face of betrayal was infectious. A murmur of agreement ran through them, the hum growing louder, becoming a determined roar.

A few hours later, Ashe found herself in the presence of another ally, Braum, the Heart of Freljord. His towering figure and warm smile were a welcoming sight. The man was a legend in Freljord, known for his mighty strength and kind heart.

"Do not worry, Ashe," he said, a comforting hand on her shoulder, "We stand by you. Betrayal or not, we are one."

His words felt like a warm drink on a cold night, comforting and encouraging. Ashe nodded, her resolve strengthening further. The road to retribution was going to be harsh and unyielding, just like the Freljord's terrain. Yet, with allies like Braum, she felt ready to face it.

"Thank you, Braum," she said, her voice echoing with newfound determination, "We'll rise from this stronger than before."

The stage was set for the Avarosans to rally their forces and return to the battle with renewed vigor. They had been struck a heavy blow, but they were far from defeated. The traitors would have to face the wrath of the united Avarosans, and the Frost Archer herself.

Alliances Shattered and Formed

Across the vast landscape of Runeterra, the bitter winds of war carried whispers of treachery and rumours of unexpected camaraderie. Old alliances, once believed to be as solid as the bedrock, crumbled under the strain of conflict. Yet, out of the ashes of broken bonds, new partnerships were taking shape, born out of shared necessity and common enemies.

In Noxus, Darius, the Hand of Noxus, found himself facing a conundrum. An ally of his, Swain, had always been a reliable and strategic partner. Yet, recent events had forced Darius to question Swain's loyalties. There were whispers, rumours of secret meetings and undisclosed alliances. His once trusted ally was now a source of suspicion.

"I trusted you, Swain," Darius found himself saying in the privacy of his war chamber, the burning torches casting long shadows on the walls. He didn't want to believe it, but the evidence was starting to mount. His hand tightened around the handle of his axe, the cold metal a harsh reminder of the realities of war.

Meanwhile, far from the militant streets of Noxus, an unlikely alliance was taking shape in the sunny city-state of Piltover. Caitlyn, the Sheriff of Piltover, and Jayce, the Defender of Tomorrow, found themselves working together, their differences put aside for the greater good. Piltover needed them to stand together, and they were not ones to back down from their duty.

Caitlyn, with her hat tipped low, eyed Jayce as he meticulously adjusted his Mercury Hammer. His actions were precise, his focus unwavering. She was still unsure of the man, his brash personality often clashing with her strict adherence to order. But there was no denying the commitment he showed to Piltover.

"We may not see eye to eye on many things, Jayce," Caitlyn said, breaking the silence between them, "But we both want what's best for Piltover."

Jayce looked up, a hint of a smile playing on his lips. "Agreed, Sheriff," he replied, his voice carrying a newfound respect for Caitlyn, "Let's show them what we can do together."

As the shadow of war loomed over Runeterra, alliances were being tested, and new ones were being forged. These shifting dynamics would be key in the battles to come. Only time would tell which of these alliances would stand strong, and which would falter under the weight of conflict.

The Void Advances

The Void, that dark and terrifying abyss, was no longer a distant threat whispered about in hushed tones. It was here, spreading its terror across Runeterra, its monstrous forces wreaking havoc and overwhelming the defenses on several fronts. The ethereal landscape, once brimming with life and color, now trembled under the ever-encroaching shadow of the Void.

The City of Progress, Piltover, was no exception. The once bustling city now resonated with the chilling echoes of the Void's monstrous minions, their shrieks a horrifying symphony of despair. Enforcer Vi, her fists tightly clenched and eyes hardened with determination, stood on the city's front line.

"Keep them back!" Vi shouted over the chaos, her usually fiery hair now a subdued hue in the blighted light. She charged, fists first, into the swarm of Voidlings, her punches landing with a satisfying crunch.

Not far from Vi, Caitlyn stood perched atop a high balcony, her rifle trained on the advancing Void forces. Her shots, each one meticulously aimed, picked off Voidlings that came too close to Piltover's defenses. Her lips were set in a grim line, her usually twinkling eyes dulled by the harsh reality they were facing. "Hold on, Vi," she murmured, mostly to herself, as she sent another well-placed shot into the oncoming swarm.

In Shurima, the golden city was awash with an eerie glow as the Void's influence seeped in, tainting the gleaming sand with its monstrous shadow. Azir, the Emperor of Sands, with the Sun Disk shining behind him, rallied his sand soldiers. "Shurima shall not fall," he declared, his voice echoing through the once-vibrant city.

But even as the leaders stood firm, there was an undeniable sense of despair creeping into the hearts of the bravest warriors. The Void was a formidable enemy, its forces relentless and numerous. The beautiful world of Runeterra, with its diverse city-states and vast landscapes, was on the brink of being consumed.

Yet, in the face of this encroaching terror, the people of Runeterra fought back with everything they had. For they knew that this was not just a fight for their cities or their homes, but a fight for their very existence. The monstrous forces of the Void advanced, but so too did the courageous heart of Runeterra.

The Battle of Will

The winds of war had swept across Runeterra, leaving no stone unturned and no heart untouched. As the relentless Void threatened to swallow everything in its path, the champions knew they were heading towards a pivotal confrontation - a clash not just of swords and magic, but of wills and spirits.

The grand city of Demacia, a stronghold of order and discipline, was shrouded in a tense stillness. Inside the city's gleaming white walls, the Lux and Garen were engaged in a fervent discussion, their faces etched with grim determination.

"We can't let the Void prevail," Lux said, her usually vibrant eyes dimmed with concern. Her staff, normally a beacon of light, lay dim and dormant against the room's stone wall.

Garen, his stalwart figure backlit by the dying light filtering in through the window, nodded. "We won't," he said, his voice a rumbling echo in the quiet room. "For Demacia, we will fight until our last breath."

Meanwhile, far from the solemnity of Demacia, the raucous and chaotic city of Bilgewater was teeming with life. Despite the encroaching threat, or perhaps because of it, the people of Bilgewater were louder, fiercer, and more defiant than ever.

Standing at the edge of the dock, gazing out at the restless sea was Miss Fortune. Her fiery hair billowed around her as the salty sea breeze danced through the city. "They think they can take our city, our home," she murmured, her fingers lightly tracing the handles of her guns. "They've got another think coming."

In the icy realms of Freljord, the atmosphere was biting, and not solely due to the weather. Inside a grand ice hall, Ashe and Sejuani were locked in a heated debate. "We must stand together if we hope to survive this," Ashe implored, her icy-blue eyes burning with resolve.

Sejuani, leaning against her massive flail, met Ashe's gaze with equal intensity. "I know," she admitted, her voice echoing in the chilly hall. "And the Winter's Claw will fight alongside the Avarosan, not because I like it, but because we need it."

Across Runeterra, every city, every faction, every champion was bracing themselves for the inevitable confrontation. And amidst the darkness and despair, a spark of hope flickered - a testament to the indomitable will of Runeterra's inhabitants. This was more than a battle of weapons and magic. It was a battle of wills, a battle for their home, a battle they were determined to win.

Fall of the Titans

Underneath a vast canopy of sky, dyed crimson with the impending dusk, the battlefield echoed a silence that was as unnerving as it was sudden. This tranquility was a chilling intermission from the orchestral discord of clashing steel and battle cries that had just seconds before roared across the expansive plains at the heart of Noxus, the indomitable fortress city.

Dominating the turmoil-ridden battlefield was the colossal figure of Darius, the Hand of Noxus, a leviathan amongst men. His muscular silhouette etched a formidable figure against the dimming twilight, his massive axe, Guillotine, gleaming ominously, thirsting for the blood of foes. Yet, even mountains crumble, and the certainty of this harsh reality was brutally carved into the hearts of the onlookers as Darius, the unwavering Titan of Noxus, collapsed onto the desolate, ravaged earth.

The aftermath of his fall was deafening. Silence fell, heavy as a shroud, over the battlefield as friend and foe alike paused their combat to watch the formidable leader of Noxus wrestle against the clutches of defeat. Darius, the embodiment of Noxian strength and resilience, the champion who had never yielded, now lay prone, wounded and overpowered by the enemy.

Beyond the city's imposing stone ramparts, where the formidable walls of Noxus began to surrender to the encroaching wilderness, Katarina, the Sinister Blade, stood in stunned silence. Her emerald eyes, usually blazing with unyielding defiance and unmatched audacity, now mirrored a ghostly echo of her former self. She had witnessed the downfall of comrades, but Darius... He was the embodiment of strength, the paragon of Noxian tenacity. He was meant to be invincible.

A considerable distance from the heart of the conflict, safely out of the lethal reach of enemy weapons, Draven, the Glorious Executioner, was frozen mid-stride, his spinning axes abruptly stilled. "No..." he whispered, the word barely escaping his lips, his usual flamboyance stripped away, replaced by raw, undeniable disbelief. To him, Darius was more than just a commander, more than a respected figurehead of Noxus; Darius was his brother.

In the sun-kissed city of Shurima, far removed from the gloom of Noxus, Emperor Azir silently observed the shocking turn of events through the mystical depths of his scrying pool. The golden light that usually danced upon his regal features now cast long shadows that seemed to reflect the gloom that filled his heart. "Even the strongest of us can fall," he murmured, his voice laced with a sorrow and an unusual hint of weariness that his usually resolute demeanor seldom betrayed.

The Fall of the Titan echoed far beyond the reaches of Noxus. The news traveled on the wind, reaching the furthest corners of Runeterra - from the technologically advanced city of Piltover suspended high above the squalor of Zaun, to the royal court of Demacia ensconced within their glittering walls, and even the rugged wilderness of Freljord. It served as a chilling reminder of the capricious nature of strength, and the brutal price that this war demanded from them.

However, lain within the folds of shock and despair, a flicker of resolve ignited. The heroes of Runeterra understood that if a titan could fall, then a titan could rise anew from the ashes of defeat. This war was far from over. They hardened their hearts and steeled their spirits, preparing for the monumental battles that awaited them in this world teetering on the edge of chaos. They understood, in the game of war, the darkest hour was always just before the dawn.

A Ray of Hope

The Rune Vault of Shurima was a cavernous expanse, hidden beneath layers of sand and time. Filled with the arcane and the forgotten, it was here that Ryze had secluded himself, his brows furrowed in concentration as he studied the aged scriptures and cryptic runes etched into the cave's ancient walls.

There was an air of desperation to his actions, a hasty urgency that was a rare sight for the usually composed Rune Mage. The echoes of Darius' fall still reverberated across Runeterra and Ryze knew that time was running out. They needed a plan, a means to turn the tide. And it was here, in this repository of untamed magic and knowledge, that he hoped to find it.

In the heart of the vault, a magical circle of runes shimmered on the stone floor, its teal glow bathing the cavern in ethereal light. His fingers traced the strange symbols, ancient language of power that few in Runeterra still understood. But Ryze was not just anyone. He was a guardian of the runes, one of the few who had devoted his life to studying and containing their vast, volatile powers.

As the last echoes of his incantation faded, the runes within the circle flared to life, glowing a vibrant blue as a powerful magic sprung forth. It illuminated a grand map of Runeterra, points of arcane energy glowing in response to the activated rune circle.

"There," Ryze pointed at a convergence of arcane energy, its vibrant glow overshadowing the rest. "The Confluence of Ley Lines, a focal point of Runeterra's magical energy. If we can direct the energy there... perhaps we can use it to our advantage."

"But how do we channel such immense power?" A new voice echoed in the cavern. Lux, the Lady of Luminosity, stepped into the circle of light. Even amidst the threat of impending doom, she exuded a sense of hope, her presence as warm and comforting as the light she wielded.

Ryze turned towards her, the weight of centuries reflecting in his eyes. "That is where we will need your light, Lux. You have a unique affinity for bending and shaping light, an extension of magic. Perhaps, it could be used to channel the energy."

Lux pondered, her expression thoughtful. "It will be dangerous... the smallest miscalculation could..."

"But if it succeeds, we may have a fighting chance." Ryze cut in. He looked at Lux, his gaze stern yet not without a glimmer of hope. "It's a risk we have to take, Lux. For Runeterra."

Their shared determination kindled a spark of hope that illuminated the Rune Vault brighter than any arcane energy. Even in the face of encroaching darkness, the champions of Runeterra would stand tall. With a newfound strategy in hand, they prepared to turn the tide of war, to bring forth a dawn that seemed almost lost.

The beacon of hope had been lit, and it would not be extinguished easily. Not as long as they had the will to fight, to stand against the Void, to defend their home. The Battle for Runeterra was far from over.

The Final Plan

In the grand chambers of the Piltover Council, a gathering of extraordinary significance was underway. All across the vast city, the hum of progress had ceased, giving way to an anxious anticipation. A sense of tension was palpable in the air as representatives from various factions of Runeterra, normally engaged in their own squabbles and power plays, were united under a singular purpose: to combat the Void.

At the head of the long, oak table, a map of Runeterra was spread out, glowing points of magic highlighting the Ley Lines. Behind her usual Sheriff's hat, Caitlyn's icy eyes scanned over the detailed plan etched out, a slight furrow creasing her normally impassive brow. The sheer audacity of the plan was frightening, yet it was the only chance they had.

"We are to channel all of Runeterra's magical energy to the Confluence of Ley Lines and then, using Lux's light, direct it against the Void." Ryze's voice echoed through the silent chamber as he laid out the risky strategy. A murmur of concern rustled through the room.

"That's playing with fire, isn't it?" spoke out Ashe, her voice as cool and clear as the Freljord winds she commanded. "What happens if we can't control the power?"

"It's a risk," Ryze admitted, his eyes meeting hers, "But it's a risk we must take. It's the only chance we have to repel the Void and protect Runeterra."

"Runeterra has faced doom before and stood tall. We will do so again." Garen's voice boomed, his conviction resounding within the council chambers. His gaze shifted towards his sister, Lux, who stood near Ryze, her eyes bright with determination.

Lux met his gaze and nodded. "I will do my part, brother. For Demacia. For Runeterra." The strength in her voice was inspiring, and a wave of quiet resolve washed over the room.

Despite the overwhelming odds and the potential for catastrophe, there was a unanimous agreement. The champions of Runeterra, no matter their previous quarrels, knew they had to stand together. It was a testament to their spirit, their determination, and their will to defend their home.

As the meeting adjourned, a shared understanding passed between them all. The plan was set, the stage was ready, and the destiny of Runeterra hung in the balance. It was a colossal task, one fraught with danger and uncertainty, but they were resolved to face it. Together.

The final plan was underway. The path was filled with uncertainty, and there was no guarantee of success. Yet, amidst the encroaching darkness, the champions held onto the faintest glimmer of hope. Runeterra would stand strong, as it always had. And they would be the ones to ensure it.

The Great Betrayal

The great hall of the Piltover Council, which had once resonated with the harmonious camaraderie of the united front, now echoed with the bitter taste of betrayal.

Swain, the Master Tactician of Noxus, had always been known for his cunning and ruthless strategy. Yet no one could have anticipated the depth of his deceit. In the heat of the battle against the Void, at a moment when their unity was most needed, he had revealed his true intentions. Noxus, under his command, had turned against the rest of Runeterra.

Caitlyn's usually composed face bore a mask of shock, her blue eyes wide with disbelief. The steady hand that had never wavered in battle trembled, as she pointed an accusing finger at the imposing figure of Swain. "How... why would you do this?"

The echo of her question hung heavily in the air. A hush fell over the grand hall, only broken by the rasp of Swain's cruel laughter. His crimson eyes gleamed with a malevolent delight that chilled the blood of those who beheld him.

"I serve Noxus," he proclaimed, his voice booming across the hall. "And Noxus stands alone, above all. Not alongside lesser nations, playing savior."

The impact of Swain's betrayal was like a hammer blow. Suddenly, the united front, already dealing with the threat of the Void, had to face a civil war from within. The fragile coalition began to crack, as old grudges and disputes resurfaced, fanned by the flames of betrayal.

The lingering silence was shattered by the impassioned voice of Lux. "This... this is not the time for petty squabbles and power plays!" Her eyes shone brightly, reflecting her namesake, as she stared down the Noxian Grand General. "We face a common enemy, an enemy that seeks to destroy not just Demacia, or Piltover, or even Noxus... but all of Runeterra."

There was a moment of silence, her words hanging heavily in the air. Yet, amidst the shock and the chaos, her words, like a spark in the darkness, began to kindle a new hope. For as one ally had turned against them, many stood strong, united against the tide of darkness and deceit.

This was their home. And they would not let it fall, not to the Void, not to internal strife, and certainly not to betrayal. It was a painful lesson, a wound that cut deep, but it was also a reminder. A reminder that no matter the treachery they faced, they would stand united. For Runeterra.

The Last Stand

The plains of Shurima were bathed in the gold of a setting sun, the vast desert stretching infinitely beneath the fiery sky. This was where they would make their stand, their last stand against the encroaching Void. Their last hope to save their world, Runeterra.

The champions, each bearing the emblem of their homeland, stood side by side. They were a mosaic of Runeterra's people – from the mechanized enforcers of Piltover to the ethereal mystics of Ionia, from the hardened warriors of Freljord to the resplendent knights of Demacia. Each had a tale to tell, and now, these stories converged here, on the sands of Shurima.

Garen, the Might of Demacia, stood resolute at the front lines, his massive sword glinting in the dying sunlight. His sister, Lux, stood by him, her staff humming with arcane energy. They represented the strength and the spirit of their city, carrying the heart of Demacia with them. "Demacia will prevail," Garen spoke, his voice reverberating through the silent ranks.

Nearby, Ashe, the Frost Archer from Freljord, clenched her frost-infused bow. Her eyes met Sejuani's, the Winter's Wrath, an unspoken truce passing between them. In this moment, their rivalry didn't matter. All that mattered was Freljord's survival.

From Piltover, Caitlyn and Vi were armed and ready, their technological gear a stark contrast to the traditional weapons around them. Yet, their determination was the same, burning with the fierce resolve to protect their city from the Void's destruction.

Ryze, the Rune Mage, stood alone, a faint blue glow emanating from the ancient runes wrapped around his body. He was a reminder of their only chance, a dangerous gamble that they had no choice but to take. They would use the power of the runes against the Void, pushing it back from whence it came.

At the center of the vast assembly, Azir, the Emperor of Sands, raised his staff high. His voice echoed across the sands, filled with an unshakeable conviction. "Today, we stand united, for Runeterra!"

And as his words hung in the air, the champions steeled themselves. The stillness of the evening was shattered by a deafening roar, an unholy sound that echoed from the edge of the horizon. The Void was coming.

But so too was Runeterra, ready for their last stand.

Victory at a Cost

The gilded city of Shurima, once a radiant jewel amidst the sun-kissed dunes, now echoed with the screams and roars of an epic struggle. The air was thick with magic and the smell of scorched earth, the golden sands churned into a war-ravaged landscape bathed in an unholy purple glow - the remnants of the Void's toxic presence.

The titans of Runeterra clashed with the monstrous horde of the Void in a battle of unimaginable proportions. The earthen ground quaked, the desert winds roared, and spells of all hues lit up the twilight sky. Amidst the chaos, one figure stood firm, his blue eyes glowing with a mix of determination and weariness.

Ryze, the Rune Mage, had been at the forefront of the conflict. Every swing of his staff, every incantation he muttered, every rune he activated, he did so with the singular purpose of repelling the encroaching Void. But even as he watched the Void's forces retreat, his heart sank at the sight of the battlefield. The cost of their victory was painted in stark, bloody detail all around him.

The icy landscape of Freljord had sent two of its fiercest daughters. Ashe and Sejuani, rivals in life, now lay united in death, their bodies surrounded by broken arrows and an extinguished flame.

Demacia's Might, the formidable Garen, had fallen. His colossal sword, so often a symbol of security, now lay abandoned by his side. His sister, Lux, knelt next to him, her staff's usual glow extinguished, her sobs echoing in the eerie silence that had blanketed the area.

From Piltover, Caitlyn and Vi had fought side by side, their advanced technology laying waste to many Void creatures. Yet, the enforcers lay still now, their machinery silenced, their mission complete.

Among the fallen was Azir, the Emperor of Sands. His sun disc, a beacon of hope in Shurima, was shattered. His golden eyes were dulled in death, his reign brought to a tragic end.

"We did it, Ryze. We saved Runeterra," Lux's voice cut through the silence, her hand on his shoulder. Ryze turned to see the young mage, her eyes red-rimmed and tired, her armor battered and scarred.

"Yes, Lux," he replied, his voice barely a whisper. "But at what cost?"

As the sun set, casting long shadows over the battered champions and their fallen comrades, a grim resolve settled in their hearts. They had won the day, but their victory was marred by loss and sacrifice. The Void was repelled, but the scars it left on Runeterra - and on them - would be a constant reminder of the price they had paid.

A New Beginning
- From Ashes to Aspiration

As the dust settled on Runeterra, the magnitude of destruction laid bare by the fateful war became more apparent. Echoes of the past reverberated through the ruins, their silence as deafening as the chaos that had preceded. Yet, as dawn's first light pierced the shroud of despair, it cast an illuminating glow on the seeds of hope that were quietly taking root. Out of the ashes of loss and sacrifice, a tenacious spirit of unity and resilience emerged, kindling a fire in the hearts of the survivors.

Noxus, the formidable fortress, was now a battle-scarred landscape. Its once-intimidating facade lay in ruins, whispering tales of a fierce battle fought. Amidst this wreckage, Draven stood with an unwavering resolve. Clutching his brother's axe, he faced the remnants of his city. His voice, usually reserved for flamboyant proclamations, rang out solemnly, "We rise from these ashes. This is our new beginning. Noxus will rebuild, grander than ever."

In Demacia, the citizens mourned their losses but resolved to rebuild. The city square, usually bustling with life, was an epitaph of brave warriors who'd fallen. Lux, embodying the undying spirit of Demacia, comforted her people, her voice steady yet filled with raw emotion, "Today, we mourn. We honor those who fell for Demacia. Tomorrow, we rebuild—for them, for us."

The icy Freljord, home to hardened warriors and ancient tribes, was marked by the ghosts of a duel that had cost them their leaders. Yet, in their shared loss, the tribes found unity. A tribal elder's words, carried by the biting wind, stirred the tribesfolk, "Their spirit endures within us. We honor them by standing united, building the future they dreamed of."

In the twin cities of Piltover and Zaun, the spirit of innovation was eclipsed by the solemnity of loss. Amidst the humming machinery and intricate inventions, the portraits of Caitlyn and Vi stood as reminders of their bravery. The air was heavy with determination as the citizens resolved to rebuild their cities, bigger and better than before.

Shurima, the golden city of the desert, bore the brutal scars of battle. But amidst the ruins, Azir's faithful followers were already laying the foundation of a new beginning. Encouraged by stories of their fallen emperor, a young servant girl announced, her voice trembling yet resolute, "Shurima will rise again, resplendent in its glory, a beacon of our spirit that never falters."

Despite the profound losses and deep scars, the spirit of Runeterra was unbroken. The people began the slow, painstaking process of rebuilding, fueled by their resilience and the promise of a brighter future. This was their new beginning—a solemn pledge of unity, strength, and a renaissance of their land.

As the wounds of Runeterra began to heal, a new chapter beckoned. Whispers of an unexplored realm beyond their borders spread amongst the champions. This new land, rich with mysteries and untapped powers, posed an exciting challenge for the champions and their people. The embers of a new adventure began to glow, suggesting a thrilling saga on the horizon. But even as this new beginning sparked hope, a disturbance rippled across the lands. A call to a journey that beckoned some of the bravest among them. As the echoes of the past slowly receded, Runeterra stood on the brink of a new dawn, a new adventure, and an untold saga that lay ahead.

Epilogue
Echoes of a Past, Whispers of a Future

As the rays of the setting sun cast a golden glow across Runeterra, the echoes of the monumental struggle that had just transpired still hung heavily in the air. The worn-out battlements bore the scars of the battle, a stark reminder of the war's devastation and the sacrifice made by so many brave champions. Yet, amidst the vestiges of the past, an undeniable spirit of hope and resilience began to stir, kindling a new flame in the hearts of the survivors.

In Noxus, Darius's monument stood as a silent testament to the city's iron will and the heavy price it had paid. Draven, his heart heavy with loss but determined, wielded his brother's axe, promising a stronger, more formidable Noxus.

In the hallowed halls of Demacia, a statue of Garen, the Might of Demacia, was unveiled, serving as a beacon of strength and unity for the Demacians. Lux, her eyes shining with unwavering resolve, pledged to rebuild Demacia, stronger and brighter than ever.

Freljord, its icy plains now a burial ground for many, was a poignant symbol of the war's cruelty. Yet, the spirit of Ashe and Sejuani lived on, uniting the tribes and inspiring a newfound unity among the people.

Piltover and Zaun, despite their significant losses, were teeming with innovation and progress. Guided by the memories of Caitlyn and Vi, the cities of progress worked tirelessly towards a brighter, more prosperous future.

Shurima, under the careful stewardship of Azir's loyal servants, was slowly regaining its former grandeur. The golden city, rising from the ashes, was a fitting emblem of Runeterra's indomitable spirit.

As Runeterra began to heal and rebuild, unsettling reports of strange disturbances from uncharted regions began to trickle in.

Twisted Fate, the Card Master, sat at the tavern in Bilgewater, listening to tales of peculiar happenings and whisperings of a new prophecy. His eyes, though weary, gleamed with a hint of anticipation. "Looks like it ain't quite over yet," he murmured, flipping a card ominously.

Twisted Fate, with his enigmatic cards and his unmatched cunning, found himself at the center of this new quest. The Card Master was no stranger to the capricious nature of fortune, and as his fingers danced along the edges of his infamous deck, he knew the road ahead would test every ounce of his skill and resolve.

Ryze, the Rune Mage, with centuries of wisdom etched in his azure skin, bore the responsibility of guiding his fellow champions. The labyrinthine catacombs of his memory held secrets and knowledge of ancient Runes that would prove crucial in their understanding of the Void.

Nami, the Marai Tidecaller, found her heart swelling with a sense of purpose. Her kin had long since held tales of the terrifying depths, of abyssal creatures beyond comprehension. Her intimate knowledge of the ocean's uncharted depths would become an invaluable asset in their quest.

Ahri, the Nine-Tailed Fox, felt the stirrings of curiosity and adventure. Her nature, inherently tied to magic and spirituality, gave her a unique perspective. Her connection to the spirit world could possibly serve as a beacon, guiding them through the shadowed paths that lay ahead.

A new era was on the horizon, a time of exploration and discovery. The champions stood at the precipice of an adventure that could potentially reshape their understanding of the cosmos, their understanding of the Void. The imminent journey was a testament to their resilience, their tenacity, and their unyielding will to protect their home. Their quest was to delve into the unknown, to seek answers to the Void's ancient riddle, and to ensure the survival and prosperity of their world, Runeterra.

The seeds of this quest had been planted. All that remained was for them to step forth into the unknown, and find a way to illuminate the darkness. After all, they were the champions of Runeterra, and there was no challenge too great, no mystery too profound. For their people, for their land, they would delve into the origins of the Void, no matter what the cost.

PART 2
Journey to the Void

A Gathering of Champions

- Under a sky painted with hues of a retiring sun, a peculiar group of individuals found themselves congregating at the heart of the Great Barrier, a majestic mountain range marking the edge of the civilized world. They were champions hailing from different corners of Runeterra - Twisted Fate, the Card Master; Ryze, the Rune Mage; Nami, the Tidecaller; and Ahri, the Nine-Tailed Fox.

Despite their distinct backgrounds, they shared a common purpose; they were about to embark on a daring journey into the enigmatic Void. The mission was perilous, the outcome uncertain, but the weight of their resolve remained unwavering.

Twisted Fate, his scarlet coat billowing slightly in the breeze, cast a roguish grin around the small group. "Well, ain't this a fancy gathering," he remarked, a deck of ornate cards dancing between his nimble fingers.

Ryze, blue skin marked with intricate tattoos that pulsated with arcane energy, merely offered him a stern nod. The mage had centuries of wisdom in his gaze, and beneath the stoic facade, there was an evident worry. "This is no time for levity, Fate. The Void...it's a place of chaos and terror. We must approach this with utmost caution."

The Rune Mage's sobering reminder settled over the group like a chilly wind. Nami, the Marai Tidecaller, shifted uncomfortably, her sapphire scales shimmering in the fading light. The ocean's whispers had spoken of the Void's horrors, stories that had left even the most courageous Marai shaken. However, as she glanced at her companions, she felt a surge of determination. "Our people trust us. We won't let them down."

Ahri, the ethereal Nine-Tailed Fox, looked from one face to the next, her heterochromatic eyes glowing with a mix of curiosity and anticipation. A soft smile played on her lips as she moved a strand of hair from her face, her nine fox tails swishing in harmony. "Indeed, we'll face this together," she said, a melodic echo of unity.

Their commitment hung in the air, a silent oath against the backdrop of the star-lit mountains. The setting was serene, a stark contrast to the turmoil they knew awaited them. A gust of wind rustled the leaves, as though the land itself was whispering a silent prayer for their success.

Each champion carried the hope of their people, the stories of their land, and the will to confront the terror of the Void. The enormity of their task was overwhelming, but the camaraderie they shared brought solace. They were ready to face the shadows, ready to unveil the mysteries of the Void.

And so, under the cloak of nightfall, the champions stood tall, their hearts echoing a single, resonating thought.

Let the journey begin.

The Reluctant Guide

Underneath the jewelled canvas of the night, four figures stood silhouetted against the ember glow of a solitary fire. The flames flickered and danced, casting odd, monstrous shadows on the rocky walls of the Great Barrier, while the champions stared into the heart of the fire, each lost in their own world of thoughts.

Ryze, the Rune Mage, was a portrait of silent contemplation. His deeply etched tattoos pulsated dimly with arcane energy, reflecting off his concerned cobalt eyes. The formidable, bearded scholar was torn between the necessity of their quest and the ghastly perils it held. The Void was a Pandora's Box, and he dreaded what terrors they might unleash in their pursuit of knowledge.

He felt a soft touch on his shoulder, pulling him out of his musings. Nami, the Marai Tidecaller, looked at him, her teal eyes mirroring his own fears. Her voice was as soothing as the rhythmic lull of ocean waves. "You've been quiet, Ryze. What worries you?"

Ryze sighed, the weight of centuries in his voice. "The Void is not just a place, Nami. It's a chaotic entity, filled with creatures of unspeakable horror. I... I fear the danger we put ourselves in."

Nami met his gaze, her expression firm yet compassionate. "We understand the risks, Ryze. We are prepared."

A chuckle broke through the serious atmosphere. Twisted Fate leaned casually against a boulder, his cards flashing in the firelight as he shuffled them with practiced ease. "Prepared? Darlin', you can never be prepared enough for the Void."

Ahri glanced at the Card Master, a teasing smile on her face. "Always the optimist, aren't you, Fate?"

Fate flashed her a wink, his easy-going persona a stark contrast to Ryze's grave concern. "Well, we won't know until we dive in, will we?"

Ahri's smile widened. "Indeed, we won't."

Ryze, silent till now, drew a deep breath, his gaze locked onto the flickering fire. He knew they were right. The time for hesitation had passed. The Void beckoned, and they had to answer its call. He finally nodded, his decision made. "Let's hope we don't dive too deep," he mused aloud, more to himself than his companions.

With their guide's acceptance, a new wave of resolve settled over the champions. The fireside murmured with whispers of anticipation and, oddly enough, camaraderie. Tomorrow, they would step into the unknown. But tonight, beneath the countless stars of Runeterra, they had each other. And perhaps, in the face of looming uncertainty, that was enough.

Abyssal Tidings

As dawn's first light began to tickle the horizon, Nami found herself staring into the steady rhythm of the ocean. The sea had always been a solace, her sanctuary amidst the turbulent storms of life. Today, however, the usually comforting dance of the waves seemed ominous, foretelling of the vast, chaotic abyss they were soon to face.

With a deep breath, she turned to face her fellow champions who sat in quiet anticipation. The Marai Tidecaller had tales to share, tales of the Void that had been passed down through generations.

Ryze, his eyes reflecting the dawning light, nodded at her. "Nami, it is time."

She took a seat on a nearby rock, the sound of crashing waves in the backdrop. She let the ocean's rhythm guide her words, her voice taking on the lilting quality of a haunting siren song.

"Our ancestors spoke of the Void with hushed whispers and bated breaths. It was a tale of darkness, of chaos, of unspeakable horror."

Her tail flicked restlessly against the rocky surface, her eyes distant as they braved the terror of yesteryears. "The Void was where light died, where sanity crumbled, where existence as we know it was devoured. It was an entity, hungry and relentless."

Ahri, her ears twitching at the grim narrative, felt a chill pass down her spine. "Yet, we choose to delve into this darkness, Nami."

The Tidecaller looked at the Nine-Tailed Fox, her teal eyes reflecting an eerie calm. "Yes, we do. Not out of ignorance, but necessity. For we can no longer turn a blind eye."

Twisted Fate shuffled his deck, the soft sound of cards strangely comforting amidst the grim conversation. "So, we face the monster head-on, eh?" he asked, his voice laced with a bravado he did not feel.

Nami simply nodded, her gaze returning to the horizon that was now bathed in the golden hue of dawn. Her voice, when it came, was softer but resolute. "We face the monster, yes. But remember, every monster was once something less terrifying. Every horror has a beginning."

Ryze looked thoughtful at her words, his mind grappling with the implications. The quest for the origin of the Void seemed more pressing than ever. They had a daunting task ahead, full of uncertainties and danger. Yet, as the new day dawned, bringing with it a strange sense of hope, the champions felt ready to meet whatever horrors awaited them.

For the Void called, and they would answer.

Spiritual Connections

With the camp settled for the night, a blanket of stars stretched above them, winking into existence as the night unfurled its inky wings. Ahri, the Nine-Tailed Fox, sat separate from the others, her golden eyes reflecting the celestial ballet unfolding overhead. The spirits called to her, a siren song only she could hear, their whispers carried on the breath of the wind.

She had always been a conduit, a bridge between the physical world and the spiritual realm. Tonight, her unique connection could potentially give them insight into the enigmatic Void, a glimpse into the heart of the darkness that they were venturing towards.

"Ahri," Ryze's voice drifted over, soft yet audible, "Are you ready?"

Her ears flicked in his direction, the multitude of tails swaying rhythmically behind her. With a nod, she closed her eyes, reaching out with her senses, letting the spiritual energies envelop her. The world around her started to recede, replaced by the ethereal hum of the spirit world.

Meanwhile, Twisted Fate and Nami watched from a distance, their faces lit by the flickering fire between them. The Card Master twirled an ornate card between his fingers, his gaze shifting between Ahri and the flames. "This is a gamble, ain't it?"

Nami replied with a soft murmur, her gaze never leaving Ahri. "Every step we take towards the Void is a gamble, Twisted Fate."

Back in her spiritual communion, Ahri found herself standing amidst a swirling vortex of spectral energy. Wisps of essence drifted around her, each a life once lived, a story once told.

"I seek guidance," she voiced to the spirits, her words echoing through the spectral plane. "We journey towards the Void, the heart of the chaos. What lies in wait for us?"

The spirits around her danced like starlight on water, each a mere flicker but collectively casting an ethereal glow. As they swirled, the murmurs of the long departed coalesced into a chorus, a harmonious symphony that seemed to resonate with the very fibers of her being. The air around her seemed to thrum with the echoes of ancient tales and forgotten truths, whispers of existence beyond the mortal plane.

From the whirling maelstrom of spiritual energy, a formless cloud began to emerge, nebulous and wavering. It churned with colors unseen by mortal eyes, an otherworldly palette of shifting hues that ebbed and flowed like the tides of the sea. Slowly, and with a sense of inexorable gravity, the cloud started to solidify, painting an image of such profound terror it sent ripples of cold dread cascading down Ahri's spine.

The image unveiled a nightmare – a tableau of the Void itself. It was an abyss, an endless expanse of darkness as black as the heart of the night. Yet, within its suffocating emptiness, life – of a sort – prevailed. Strange, twisted creatures prowled the Void's desolate landscapes, each a distorted echo of the natural order of things. Their forms were warped and contorted, testament to the chaotic nature of their unholy birthplace. Grotesque parodies of life, they stood as chilling reminders of the terrifying power that the Void possessed.

Yet, amidst the chaotic and malevolent beauty of the Void, Ahri discerned a certain rhythm, a cryptic pattern that seemed to pulse through the lifeforms and landscapes. It was akin to a heartbeat, a throbbing pulse that underpinned the Void's existence. A startling revelation began to dawn upon Ahri. The Void, for all its chaos and terror, might not be as senseless as it seemed.

In that moment, as she stood at the precipice of understanding, the Void ceased to be just an unending abyss of chaos. It became a complex enigma waiting to be solved, a challenge that they must surmount for the survival and prosperity of Runeterra.

As Ahri emerged from the spiritual communion, her golden eyes flared with a newfound determination. The Void was a mystery, an enigma. But it wasn't insurmountable

With her fellow champions at her side, she felt a flicker of hope. For they were the torchbearers in this journey into darkness, and they would illuminate the Void.

Mapping the Unknown

The low murmur of conversation filled the musty air of the makeshift war room, a stark contrast to the silent mystery of the Void that loomed over them. A large wooden table stood in the centre, strewn with ancient texts, arcane diagrams and, at the center of it all, a map. A map of a place that existed beyond the confines of their world, a vast, mysterious expanse known only as the Void.

At the head of the table, Ryze hovered over an aged tome, its pages yellowed and brittle with age. His azure eyes, luminescent against his dark, runic skin, flickered with concentration. Every now and then, he would glance towards the map and point, his movements precise, methodical.

Nami watched him, her bright eyes reflecting the flickering candlelight. She absentmindedly ran her fingers over the nacreous scales on her tail, a nervous habit she had picked up ever since they started their mission. Her gaze turned towards the map, lingering over the place where her home, the oceanic abyss, met the unending darkness of the Void. Her mind was filled with the ancient tales of her people, cautionary whispers of monstrous creatures and dreadful silence that lingered in the Void.

Twisted Fate leaned against a wall, flipping his cards with an effortless rhythm. The rhythmic sound of his cards shuffling was a strange comfort amidst the tension. He watched his companions, his eyes as inscrutable as the Card Master himself. He caught Nami's gaze and gave her a reassuring wink. This was a gamble like no other, but it was a gamble they had to take.

Ahri sat a little apart from the rest, her nine tails flickering like wisps of fire. Her golden eyes were distant, lost in the spectral conversation she had had with the spirits. The glimpse of the Void was still fresh in her mind, an ink-blot stain on her consciousness.

"The path will be treacherous," Ryze broke the silence, his voice carrying a weight that temporarily cleared the room of its foreboding aura. He traced a jagged line through the center of the map. "And the Void itself will resist our intrusion. But we must persist."

Nami nodded, her grip tightening on her staff. Twisted Fate simply tipped his hat, his fingers never stopping their dance over his deck of cards. Ahri turned her gaze from the flickering fire to the map, a new determination in her eyes.

"Our journey starts now," Ryze announced, his hand resting on the map's edge. "Into the unknown, for Runeterra."

The words hung heavy in the room, echoing off the stone walls and solidifying their resolve. Together, they faced an unpredictable abyss. Together, they would illuminate the Void, chart the unknown, and bring light to the darkest corners of their reality. The echoes of war still rang in their ears, but it was time for a new story. One of exploration, of discovery, of understanding.

The next chapter of their saga was about to begin.

A Shadowed Path

The dawn had not yet broken over the vast landscape of Runeterra as four figures stood at the precipice of the unknown, the Void's outskirts. The boundary where their world met the abyss was not marked by a physical line but was more of an unnerving sensation, a feeling of cold dread that seemed to permeate the air.

Twisted Fate stood at the forefront, his signature hat tipped back as he surveyed the dark expanse. His usual playful demeanor had been replaced with a more contemplative one. He flicked a card between his fingers, the glinting object slicing through the quiet tension of the morning.

Ryze stood beside him, his eyes locked on the arcane scroll clutched in his hands. The ancient parchment was filled with runes, their mysterious glow illuminating his stern face. His azure eyes held a sense of gravitas, a silent understanding of the enormity of their undertaking.

Nami was a few steps back, her staff firmly planted in the ground. The Tidecaller's usually vibrant blue eyes mirrored the unease that filled the air. Yet beneath the apprehension was a determination forged from countless tales of courage and resilience of her Marai ancestors.

A few paces away, Ahri sat in a meditative pose, her nine tails flickering around her like ethereal flames. The Nine-Tailed Fox was a study in quiet concentration, her mind connected to the myriad of spirits that surrounded them.

"Are we all ready?" Ryze's voice cut through the silence, his gaze shifting from the scroll to his fellow champions. They nodded in response, each one feeling the weight of the mission ahead.

"I must admit," Twisted Fate began, his voice steady despite the uncertainty that lay ahead. "I've played against high stakes before, but this is a whole new deck."

The Card Master's attempt at levity eased some of the tension, and a faint smile crossed Nami's face. "We face this together," she stated, her voice carrying the echoes of the Marai's age-old wisdom.

Ahri opened her eyes, a spectral glow emanating from them. "The spirits are with us," she confirmed, the quiet confidence in her voice grounding them.

With one last collective breath, they stepped into the shadowed path, leaving the familiarity of their world behind. The chilling unknown of the Void stretched out before them, an abyssal puzzle waiting to be unraveled.

As the first rays of dawn touched Runeterra, the champions had already embarked on their journey, walking a path shadowed by mysteries and ominous silence. They carried with them not just the hopes of their people, but also the unwavering resolve to illuminate the Void and bring understanding to the very darkness that threatened their world.

The Void's Resistance

The chilling landscape of the Void was a stark contrast to the vibrant world of Runeterra. Instead of the familiar greenery and life that filled their homeland, they were met with a wasteland of darkness, broken only by the twisted, alien formations that jutted from the barren ground.

Ryze gripped his scroll tighter, the glowing runes reflecting in his azure eyes. Twisted Fate flicked a card restlessly between his fingers, his face a mask of concentration. Nami clutched her staff, the energy at its tip pulsing in response to the foreboding atmosphere. Ahri's nine tails flickered around her as she attuned herself to the strange energy surrounding them.

Their cautious advance was halted as a horrifying screech tore through the oppressive silence. Emerging from the blackened soil came a group of creatures so alien and grotesque they defied description. Their forms seemed to shift and ripple as though not entirely fixed in this reality. Their very existence seemed an affront to nature.

Twisted Fate grimaced, pulling a card from his deck. "I've never been a fan of cheaters," he declared, his voice laced with determination. With a flick of his wrist, the card soared towards the creatures, glowing with potent energy.

Ryze stepped forward, his voice resonating with arcane power as he chanted incantations. Streams of glowing runes erupted from the scroll, forming a protective barrier around the champions. Nami raised her staff, calling forth a tidal wave that crashed against the barrier, ready to sweep away anything that threatened to breach it.

Ahri's tails pulsed with energy, and she reached out with her senses, trying to communicate with the hostile entities. "We mean no harm," she murmured, her voice echoing in the desolate surroundings. But her plea was met with an intensified assault on their barrier.

As the first Void creature lunged, Twisted Fate snapped his wrist, throwing his card with deadly precision. It arced through the air, bursting into a vibrant shower of energy upon impact. The creature recoiled, but more were surging forward, closing the gap with terrifying speed.

Ryze, however, was ready. His scroll unfurled, the arcane script glowing with a fierce light. As his resonant voice called out ancient incantations, the runes swirled around them, forming an impenetrable barrier. The Void creatures crashed against the magical shield like a tide against a cliff, but the barrier held firm, an island of hope amidst the sea of chaos.

Nami stood tall behind Ryze's shield, her staff raised high. The gem at the peak pulsed with a gentle light, a stark contrast to the harsh, dark hues of the Void. With a forceful downward motion, a colossal tidal wave burst into existence, sweeping towards their enemies. The water clashed against the Void creatures, slowing their assault and sowing disarray in their ranks.

Ahri, her nine tails aglow with magical energy, attempted to bridge a connection. She reached out with her senses, touching the minds of the hostile entities. Her plea echoed through the battle: "We mean no harm." It was met with confusion, then a palpable surge of aggression. It seemed communication was off the table.

Undeterred, Ahri joined her comrades in the fight. Her hands drew together, forming a pulsating orb of energy. With a graceful movement, she released it, the orb flying forward and exploding amongst the Void creatures, causing them to scatter.

The battle was a maelstrom of sound and light, a clash of Runeterra's finest against the eldritch horrors of the Void. Energy crackled and popped, the ground quaked, and the air filled with the roar of elemental magic and the screeches of Void creatures.

Through it all, the champions stood their ground. Despite the chaos swirling around them, they moved with purpose and unity, a singular force amidst the tumult. Each spell cast, each card thrown, each wave summoned was a defiant assertion of their will, a testament to their determination. They were the champions of Runeterra, and they would not be turned away from their mission.

They faced their first major hurdle within the Void, the champions realized the extent of the challenge they had taken upon themselves. But even amidst the ferocious onslaught, their spirits did not falter. They were the champions of Runeterra, and they would not be easily thwarted. Their resolve solidified with every hostile encounter, their determination burning brighter against the stark backdrop of the abyss.

Unexpected Aid

Before the Champions could rejoice from their first fight a second wave approached them from the rear. The relentless Void creatures surged, a dark tide beneath an even darker sky. Amidst this bleak landscape, the champions stood as a beacon of defiance. Magic crackled and sparked around them, their determined faces illuminated in the stark glow of the runes, the vibrant splash of Twisted Fate's cards, the soft radiance of Nami's staff, and the nine-tailed light of Ahri.

Suddenly, a new force joined the fray. From the shadows stepped a figure, swathed in tattered cloaks that seemed to shimmer and ripple with an otherworldly energy. His eyes, a penetrating purple, shone with an intensity that could only be born of personal vendetta.

"Kassadin," Ryze breathed, recognizing the new arrival, "The Voidwalker."

The Void creatures seemed to react to Kassadin's presence, their guttural cries reaching a fevered pitch. Undeterred, Kassadin brandished a wickedly sharp blade, crafted from the very substance of the Void itself, and charged into battle.

Kassadin's attacks were brutal and precise. He weaved in and out of the enemy ranks, his movements so swift and fluid they were barely discernible. With each strike, a Void creature fell, dissipating into nothingness. His mastery over the Void was unmistakable, his determination a powerful tide pushing back against the relentless surge of the Void's minions.

Watching him, Twisted Fate couldn't help but feel a twinge of awe. "Never thought I'd be glad to see him," he murmured, flinging a card that exploded in a burst of light and energy against an oncoming creature.

Nami nodded, her eyes wide as she observed the Voidwalker. "We have to use this opportunity. Push forward!"

Ahri, her ears perked in attention, agreed. "Right. Follow my lead."

United, they pressed on, their renewed vigor invigorating the battlefield. With the unexpected aid of Kassadin, the tide seemed to turn in their favor. The Void creatures began to retreat, their screeches echoing hauntingly across the desolate landscape.

As the final creature faded into the obscurity of the Void, Kassadin turned to face the champions. "I walk the path of the Void to seek vengeance, not to make allies," he said, his voice cold yet resonant. "But it seems our goals align...for now."

Despite the harshness of his words, the champions found solace. For in the dark abyss of the Void, they had found an unlikely ally, and perhaps, a glimmer of hope.

The Voidwalker's Tale

The heroes and their newfound ally found themselves camped under an eerily beautiful Void sky, its ethereal, pulsating lights a stark contrast to the ominous blackness surrounding them. Huddled around a swirling, magical flame conjured by Ryze, the team settled into an uneasy rest, every one of them on edge in the heart of the unknown.

Kassadin, the Voidwalker, stood apart, his gaze affixed to the dancing Void lights above. His silence was as tangible as the chill that swept the Void lands, yet there was an unspoken agreement among the champions that he held vital knowledge about their path ahead.

"Your help was unexpected, Kassadin," Ryze started, breaking the silence, his azure eyes fixed on the brooding figure. "What brings you to aid us?"

Kassadin turned slowly to face them, his eyes a mirror of the Void's eerie lights. "The Void took everything from me," he said, his voice a haunting echo in the empty expanse. "My home, my family, my life. I walk the Void not for redemption, but for revenge."

As he spoke, the chilling detachment in his voice melted away, replaced by a raw, aching grief that resonated with the champions. For all their differences, they were united in their understanding of loss, having borne witness to the devastation the Void and other evils had brought to Runeterra.

"I never chose to guide anyone," Kassadin continued, "But your presence here... it could change things. We share a common enemy."

His words hung in the air as the champions considered his story. Despite the horrors Kassadin had faced, his will remained unbroken, his resolve unyielding. In him, they saw a reflection of their own determination - a shared commitment to protect Runeterra at all costs.

Nami was the first to respond, her usually vibrant voice softened with empathy. "Your pain is a burden no one should bear alone, Kassadin. We are with you in this fight."

Kassadin gave a slight nod, his stony countenance softening ever so slightly. Perhaps, amidst the terrifying unknown of the Void, this unusual gathering of champions had sparked a flicker of camaraderie.

As the magical fire waned, the group settled in for the night, each lost in their thoughts. Their journey had just begun, but they now had a deeper understanding of the Void and what they were fighting against. And perhaps most importantly, they realized they weren't alone in their battle.

Their determination steeled, the champions looked ahead to the challenges and revelations the Void would surely throw their way. Guided by Kassadin, they knew they were a step closer to unraveling the mysteries of the Void and ensuring the safety of their beloved Runeterra.

The Echoes of the Past

The following day's journey led them deeper into the chilling expanse of the Void, its monotonous landscape now punctuated by eerie, twisted structures that hinted at a forgotten civilization. The ruins bore a strange, unsettling beauty - architectural marvels warped by the Void's insidious touch, a haunting testament to a swallowed past.

The team approached the ruins cautiously, their curiosity tinged with a pervasive sense of dread. The twisted edifices loomed over them, casting long, strange shadows on the ghostly landscape. "A reminder of the Void's destruction," Kassadin muttered, his voice as hollow as the abandoned structures.

Despite the eerie atmosphere, Ahri's eyes sparkled with a mix of apprehension and excitement. "These ruins... they're not just wreckage. They're a piece of history, a clue about the nature of the Void," she declared, her nine tails swaying with her enthusiasm.

Twisted Fate tossed a card into the air, watching it twist and turn before deftly catching it. "Let's hope they're a clue to getting us out of here when the time comes," he retorted, the playful sarcasm failing to mask his underlying concern.

Nami, always sensitive to her surroundings, moved closer to one of the towering structures. Her aquatic features rippled with an unfamiliar sense of discomfort. "The energy here is... disturbed. Unsettled," she reported, her voice echoing eerily in the desolate expanse.

As they ventured deeper into the abandoned city, they stumbled upon a mural, untouched by the Void's corruption. It was a breathtaking depiction of a civilization once teeming with life, a stark contrast to the desolate cityscape around them.

Ryze, ever the scholar, studied the mural intently. "These markings... They speak of a great calamity, an abyss devouring the stars.

A prophecy, perhaps," he mused, his mind whirling with theories and conjectures.

The realization was as chilling as the Void's cold grip - they were walking through a ghost town, a victim of the Void's insatiable hunger. This civilization had faced what Runeterra might if they failed.

Silently, they made their way through the ruins, each lost in their thoughts. The past echoed around them, whispering tales of the Void's terror. The journey was far from over, the path ahead filled with trepidation, but the champions held on, united by a resolve forged in the crucible of their shared experiences. They had a mission to complete, a world to save, and they would face the abyss together.

The Frozen Watchers

As they ventured further into the alien landscape, a chilling gust swept across the plain, carrying a voice that echoed hauntingly in their minds. "Champions, heed my call."

Turning towards the source of the voice, they found a figure emerging from a shimmering portal of ice. It was Lissandra, the Ice Witch of Freljord, her presence as cold and commanding as the wintry realm she governed.

"I require your assistance," she stated, her voice laced with a desperate urgency that belied her stoic demeanor.

Ryze, his distrustful gaze fixed on the Ice Witch, responded curtly, "Our path lies towards the heart of the Void, not Freljord."

But Lissandra's frost-rimed eyes held a silent plea. "A new threat stirs in the depths of the Howling Abyss. The Watchers - ancient entities from the Void itself - threaten to emerge once more. If we don't stop them, your quest will be for naught."

In the ensuing silence, Twisted Fate shuffled his cards nervously. "Sounds like a gamble either way."

Ahri, ever the diplomat, stepped forward. "If the Void threatens Freljord, it threatens us all. We'll aid you, Lissandra."

Guided by Lissandra, they traversed a temporary portal, a rift through dimensions, emerging in the icy winds of Freljord's Howling Abyss. As they stood at the edge of the abyss, the vast expanse of darkness stared back at them, the eerie quiet punctuated only by the distant echo of the winds.

Then, the quiet was shattered as the ground rumbled beneath them. Massive, twisted figures began to rise from the abyss - the Watchers. Their forms, massive and twisted, were horrific parodies of life as it was known on Runeterra.

With a quick nod from Lissandra, the champions sprang into action. Nami's tidal waves crashed against the behemoths, Ryze's runes burned bright against the frozen landscape, and Ahri's spirit orbs danced through the frigid air. Twisted Fate deftly wove between the chaos, his cards slicing through the icy winds with deadly precision.

Ryze's arcane magic clashed with the monstrous entities, runes etching ephemeral chains into the fabric of reality, binding the lumbering creatures in place. Ahri's spirit orbs were whirling dervishes of raw energy, darting through the frost-laden air with wild abandon. Each orb that found its mark sizzled and popped against the frozen hide of the watchers, burning away portions of their form with every hit.

Nami, the Marai Tidecaller, found her natural affinity to water strengthened amidst the icy battleground. With a flick of her staff, she conjured towering waves from the frosty ether itself, crashing them down on the watchers with the wrath of an ocean tempest. Each wave's impact was an explosion of freezing water and ice shards that cut through the monstrous forms, causing them to roar in surprise and pain.

Twisted Fate, the Card Master, moved between his companions and enemies with deft ease, each card he flung biting into the monstrous watchers like a stinging hornet. The incantations imbued in the cards glowed brightly, casting a kaleidoscope of colours against the bleak whiteness of Freljord.

At the helm of their formation, Lissandra unleashed her mastery over ice and frost. With each imperious sweep of her staff, jagged ice spikes erupted from the ground, skewering the watchers, impaling them onto the very land they sought to conquer. Her eyes glowed with icy resolve as she turned the watchers' domain against them.

As the last watcher fell, impaled on a colossal spike of Lissandra's conjuring, a silence fell over the battlefield. The champions, panting and wearied, watched as the monstrous figure writhed before eventually falling still. A moment later, it crumbled, its form dispersing into a cloud of inky blackness that was quickly swallowed by the abyss. The threat, at least for now, was quelled.

A collective sigh of relief passed through the champions, their breath misting in the frigid air. Their hearts pounded in their chests, adrenaline slowly fading from their veins. They had won the battle, but the war with the Void was far from over. Their eyes met in silent understanding, the icy winds of Freljord carrying away their unspoken vows of unity and resilience.

As they returned to the Void's entry, Lissandra turned to them, her frosty countenance softening ever so slightly. "You have my gratitude, champions. Freljord is in your debt."

They stepped back into the Void, their spirits emboldened by the victory. But the encounter had been a stark reminder - the Void was a force far beyond their understanding, and their quest was only beginning.

Respite and Revelations

In the aftermath of their battle, the champions found themselves encamped in the heart of the glacial Freljord, nestled amidst towering ice pillars that reflected the shimmering auroras of the night sky. The cool glow lent a certain serenity to the surroundings, a much-needed reprieve after the tumult of their clash with the Watchers.

Despite the biting chill, a fire burned in their midst, its dancing flames casting long, flickering shadows across the icy terrain. Twisted Fate, one leg nonchalantly thrown over the other, reclined by the fire. In his hands, a deck of cards fluttered, each flip punctuated by the crackling fire.

Opposite him sat Ryze, the Rune Mage's usual stern countenance replaced by a look of deep introspection. His gaze seemed to penetrate the very heart of the fire, lost in a world of ancient lore and half-forgotten memories.

Nami and Ahri had found their spots nearby, their eyes reflecting the mesmerizing dance of the auroras above. The peacefulness of the moment belied the dangerous journey that lay ahead, a stark contrast that didn't go unnoticed.

In the hush, Twisted Fate's voice rose, surprisingly soft, "What's the first thing you plan to do when all this is over?" His gaze flitted across the group. Ryze looked up, breaking away from his reverie, Nami turned, curiosity lighting her eyes, and Ahri's ears perked up, her attention caught.

One by one, they shared their dreams, painting verbal pictures of their homelands, their people, their hopes for the future. Nami spoke of the Marai, her kin in the deep oceans, while Ahri shared her yearning to explore the spiritual realm, to comprehend her nature better. Ryze, though hesitant at first, spoke of his duty to protect the world's Runes and his desire to see a world at peace.

And as Twisted Fate shared his dream of a gamble-free life (a statement met with raised eyebrows and disbelief), they found a sense of camaraderie building between them, strengthened by shared dreams and a shared mission.

It was a quiet moment of respite, a calm before the storm. Yet, in the sharing of stories and dreams, they found not just solace, but resolve, a determination to protect their world, their home. As they each retreated into their tents, the dreams of what awaited them at the journey's end fueled their courage, gearing them up for the trials that lay ahead. After all, they weren't just fighting for themselves - they were fighting for their dreams, their people, and their world. Runeterra.

Deeper into Darkness

The Freljord's icy embrace was soon replaced by the chilling, relentless void. The difference, though, was palpable. The ice was nature's product, her frosty kiss during the world's slumber. The void, however, was unnatural, a distortion of reality, a place where the usual rules of time and space seemed to fold in on themselves.

The group advanced, their path lit by the ghostly glow of Ryze's arcane magic. Around them, the Void pulsed and writhed, an abyssal landscape where whispers seemed to echo from nowhere and shadows moved with an eerie life of their own. Twisted Fate's fingers nervously fiddled with his deck, while Nami's staff left a trail of luminescent bubbles that hung in the air before fading into the abyss.

Kassadin, their enigmatic guide, was their compass in this alien landscape. Despite his own history with the Void, there was an uncanny calmness about him, an acceptance of the surreal surroundings that was both comforting and unsettling. "We must be vigilant," he warned, his voice a low rumble that somehow carried through the Void's unnatural silence. "The deeper we go, the more twisted the inhabitants."

Ahri's tails flickered anxiously, her spirit sense tingling with a foreboding unease. "There's a dark energy here," she murmured, her eyes glowing with an ethereal light. "It's... it's different from what we've encountered before."

Just as she finished her sentence, a chilling screech echoed from the depths, a sound that seemed to claw its way into their minds, a harbinger of the horrors that lurked in the inky darkness.

"Kassadin," Twisted Fate began, his voice cutting through the omnipresent hum of the Void, "How can you stand this place? It's eerie... like a nightmare you can't wake up from."

Kassadin turned to face him, his countenance obscured by the mask he wore. "It is not about standing the Void, Twisted Fate," he said, his voice steady and deep. "It's about understanding it, learning its ebbs and flows. The Void is not just a physical entity. It's a state of mind."

Ahri's ears perked up at his words, her curiosity piqued. "A state of mind?" she asked, a trace of skepticism coloring her tone.

"Yes," Kassadin nodded, gazing into the swirling abyss around them. "To navigate the Void, you must attune yourself to its rhythm, comprehend its dissonance. To resist it is to invite disaster."

Ryze, who had been quiet, suddenly spoke up. "Resisting is what we do, Kassadin," he said, his voice echoing a long history of battles fought and knowledge acquired. "We resisted when the Rune Wars threatened to tear Runeterra apart. We resisted when the Darkin sought to enslave humanity. And we will resist now."

Kassadin was silent for a moment before answering. "And yet, here we stand," he said finally, his voice soft. "In the heart of the Void, not resisting, but seeking to understand. Perhaps, old mage, there are lessons for us all in these dark depths."

Nami, who had been silently trailing her luminous staff in the swirling abyss, finally chimed in. "Then let's learn quickly," she said, her voice bubbling with an anxious optimism. "The sooner we understand this place, the sooner we can protect our home."

Their words hung in the air, a testament to their determination. Each champion, though different in their approach, was bound by a common purpose - to understand, to learn, and to safeguard the world they held dear. And so, they pressed on, their dialogues a beacon of hope in the unforgiving landscape of the Void.

The champions steeled themselves, their resolve hardening under the all-encompassing darkness.

With a deep breath, Ryze tightened his grip on his scroll, his runic tattoos illuminating the stark landscape. "Then we face it," he declared, determination lacing his words. "For Runeterra."

The journey had just started, and already, they felt the weight of their mission, the burden of their quest. But they were champions, and they would face the darkness, armed with hope, bravery, and an unyielding commitment to their cause.

The Darkin Blade

The chilling emptiness of the Void was broken by an unexpected intrusion. A sharp, harried cry for help. It was a voice they recognized – Kayn, the Shadow Reaper. His message was scattered, torn by static, but the urgency in his voice was unmistakable. Something was wrong, terribly wrong. The Darkin Blade, Aatrox, was on a rampage.

The connection between Aatrox and the Void was a tale as old as time itself. Aatrox, one of the five remaining Darkin, was a fearsome and formidable entity, the raw power of the Void coursing through his veins, forging him into a weapon of war and destruction. And now, it seemed, the blade was out of control.

"You reckon we should help?" Twisted Fate asked, a hint of skepticism lining his tone.

Ryze was quick to respond. "Aatrox is a powerful Darkin. His link to the Void... it may hold answers we need." His voice held a grim determination, a clear indication that they would answer Kayn's call.

The champions found Kayn in a clearing, struggling to maintain control over the Darkin Blade. His eyes were wild, desperation etching lines on his young face.

"Aatrox!" Ryze called out, his voice firm. "Release Kayn!"

The Darkin turned his attention to them, a dark laugh escaping his lips. "Why should I, Rune Mage? Kayn is mine."

Ahri, her tails flickering in agitation, stepped forward. "We won't let you. We've faced far greater threats than you, Aatrox."

The ensuing battle was a blend of magic and might, the champions working in tandem to subdue Aatrox and free Kayn. They knew the cost of failure - not only would they lose a valuable ally, but they would also allow a powerful entity of the Void to run unchecked.

The sight of Nami's tidal wave crashing against Aatrox, Twisted Fate's cards whizzing through the air, Ryze's runes creating a protective barrier, and Ahri's spirit orbs illuminating the Void's dark abyss was a spectacle of unity and determination.

The fight was arduous, the Darkin not willing to give in. Yet, as the dust settled, Aatrox was subdued, his form dissipating back into the blade, leaving a breathless and worn Kayn in its wake.

The champions offered their aid, helping Kayn to his feet. While the side quest had been a detour, the insight gained from their encounter with Aatrox proved invaluable. They had discovered another layer of the Void, and though it painted an even more daunting picture, it was a step forward in their quest.

As they moved onwards, each knew that their journey was far from over. They had braved the Darkin's wrath and emerged victorious, but the Void was still an enigma, and they were only beginning to uncover its secrets.

The Clash of Darkin

The Void was a battlefield, the champions standing against the fearsome form of Aatrox, the Darkin Blade. He towered over them, his very presence a maelstrom of malevolence that seemed to suck the life out of their surroundings.

"You cannot stop me!" Aatrox boomed, his voice echoing around them. His laughter, a chilling crescendo, echoed through the bleak landscape of the Void.

"We'll see about that," Twisted Fate retorted, shuffling his cards with a nervous energy. His cavalier demeanor belied the tension in his shoulders, a telltale sign of the immense pressure they all felt.

The battle was chaotic and dangerous. Aatrox was a relentless force, his blows powerful enough to level mountains. But the champions held their ground. Ryze's magical runes danced around them, forming shields and firing spells, while Ahri weaved between the onslaught, her spirit orbs leaving trails of glowing energy as they struck the Darkin. Twisted Fate's cards were a constant barrage, their enchanted edges biting into the Darkin's armor. Nami's control over the water was a lifeline, her spells healing their injuries and buffing their defenses.

Despite the intensity of the battle, the champions couldn't help but notice the patterns within Aatrox's movements, the arcane symbols glowing ominously on the Darkin Blade. It was an eerie sight that tugged at the corners of Ryze's mind, a puzzle waiting to be unraveled.

"Aatrox," Ryze said, his voice strong despite the cacophony of the battle. "You were not always this way. You were Ascended, once, before the Void consumed you."

A bitter laugh escaped Aatrox. "Yes, Rune Mage. A 'gift' from our celestial benefactors. But the Void... it offered us true power."

This revelation hit them hard. The Darkin were not creatures born of the Void but were once Ascended, celestial beings transformed into monsters by the abyss. It was a sobering thought, a cruel reminder of the Void's corruptive influence.

The champions used this newfound knowledge, their attacks becoming more strategic, aiming for the weak spots in Aatrox's armor. The battle raged on, the Void echoing with the sounds of clashing magic and steel.

And when the dust finally settled, Aatrox was forced back into the Darkin Blade, his monstrous form dissipating in an ethereal wisp of Void energy. It was a victory, though it came with a heavy price. The champions were visibly weary, their energy spent and bodies battered.

Yet, amidst the exhaustion and pain, there was a sense of accomplishment. They had faced the Darkin and emerged victorious. They had learnt a crucial piece of history, a key that could potentially help them understand the Void better.

As they looked upon the fallen Darkin Blade, the champions knew they were one step closer to understanding the enigmatic abyss that was the Void. They had learnt a lot, but the journey was far from over. There were still secrets to uncover, mysteries to solve. And they would face them together, as champions of Runeterra.

Void's Heart

The journey into the heart of the Void was both surreal and terrifying. The further they travelled, the more the rules of their reality seemed to bend and warp. Time lost meaning, space distorted in inexplicable ways. But amidst the fear and uncertainty, there was a sense of anticipation that spurred the champions onward.

They found themselves in a realm that was a jumble of contradictions, a landscape born of chaos and alien energies. The terrain was harsh and uninviting, a vast expanse of darkness punctuated by jagged formations that seemed to pulse with an eerie light.

"What is this place?" Ahri asked, her voice echoing strangely.

Ryze gazed at the alien landscape, his eyes narrowed in concentration. "This," he said, his voice low, "is the heart of the Void."

There was an undeniable sense of power here, a pulsating force that seemed to resonate with the arcane symbols tattooed on Ryze's skin. It was a sensation that was both frightening and exhilarating.

"We're close," Nami murmured, her eyes reflecting the strange light of the Void. "Can you feel it? The energy, it's... it's different here."

Twisted Fate shuffled his deck nervously. "Yeah, I can feel it. Feels like we're walking into a den of hungry lions."

Despite the ominous setting, they pressed on, navigating the twisted landscape with grim determination. With every step, they could feel the power of the Void growing stronger, more palpable. They knew they were treading on dangerous ground, yet there was no turning back.

The heart of the Void was a sight to behold. An immense nexus of swirling energies, pulsating in rhythm to an unseen heartbeat. It was beautiful in a terrifying sort of way, an embodiment of raw, untamed power.

"This is it," Ryze said, his voice barely a whisper. "This is the source of the Void's power."

A hush fell over the group, the enormity of their journey hitting them all at once. They were standing in the heart of their enemy's territory, the source of all the pain and destruction that had befallen their world. It was a sobering realization, but also a reminder of the importance of their mission.

Lost in the Void

The tranquillity of their collective focus shattered as the ground beneath them rumbled violently. The pulsating heart of the Void flared with blinding intensity, and an overwhelming surge of energy burst forth, creating a rift that swallowed the champions whole.

When the light dimmed and the disorienting sensation subsided, each found themselves utterly alone in the desolate expanse of the Void. The familiar figures of their comrades were nowhere to be seen, replaced by a disarray of grotesque formations and disconcerting void-born creatures.

Twisted Fate found himself standing atop a tower of crystalline shards, his hand clutching his deck in an iron grip. He squinted at the alien landscape, the alien stars in the distance offering no comfort. "Well, this ain't ideal," he muttered, slipping a card between his fingers.

Ahri, stranded amidst an eerie forest of towering monoliths, swallowed the rising panic. Her tails flickered nervously, and her spiritual energy reached out instinctively, searching for the comforting presence of her friends. To her dismay, the only responses were the whispers of unseen spirits, their words indecipherable yet teeming with fear.

Meanwhile, Nami discovered herself in a vast canyon that resembled the abyssal depths of her ocean home, save for the absence of water and the strange gravity that allowed her to walk as if on land. The Tidecaller tightened her grip on her staff, her gaze stern as she began to navigate the alien terrain.

Ryze, in the midst of an endless expanse of void-touched desert, glanced down at the ancient runes inscribed on his arms. The symbols pulsed with a soft light, responding to the potent Void energy that saturated the air. The Rune Mage clenched his fists, a storm of arcane energy crackling around him.

Isolated but undeterred, each champion steeled their resolve. This was but another test, another obstacle to overcome on their quest to unravel the secrets of the Void. Even separated, they were a team, and they would find a way to regroup.

As they ventured deeper into their respective sections of the Void, they held on to the memories of camaraderie, of shared goals and shared fears. Each step, each battle, each encounter with the Void's grotesque creations only strengthened their determination.

They were the champions of Runeterra, lost but never defeated. Despite the insurmountable odds, they pressed on, their spirits indomitable, their resolve unbreakable. The Void might have swallowed them whole, but they would not let it consume them. They would reunite, they would fight, and they would overcome.

A Race Against Time

In the midst of the Void's desolate vastness, time became an enigma. The rhythmic ticking of a clock was replaced by the cacophony of alien sounds that echoed in the abyss. Yet, each champion felt a relentless pressure, an urgency that gnawed at their courage, the race against time had begun.

Twisted Fate, atop his crystalline tower, squinted at the distant horizon, his card hovering at his side, spinning lazily. He pulled his hat lower, shadowing his eyes. "Don't reckon we've got much time, partner," he said, addressing the card as if it were a sentient being. With a determined nod, he descended the tower, his every move calculated to conserve time and energy.

Ahri, encased within the eerie monoliths, traced her fingers along the smooth surface of a stone structure. Her other hand clutched her orb, its pale light providing a small measure of comfort. "I hope you're all safe," she whispered, her voice barely audible above the low hum of the Void. Her eyes flashed with resolve as she darted forward, swift as the wind, her mind focused on finding her allies.

Amidst her canyon-like surroundings, Nami raised her staff, its tip glowing with ethereal blue light. "Time and tide wait for no one," she muttered, the proverbial words of her people taking on a literal meaning in her current predicament. She began to move, her form gliding across the terrain as if she were swimming against a powerful current.

Ryze, standing amidst the endless desert, felt the pulse of his runes growing faster, like a heartbeat responding to adrenaline. The desert before him stretched into infinity, but he knew better than to be intimidated by the size of a task. "One step at a time," he murmured, his voice a quiet rumble amidst the desert's silence. With an unreadable expression, he began his march, his arcane energy wrapping around him like a protective shroud.

Their solitary journeys through the abyss were punctuated by encounters with void-born creatures, each confrontation a stark reminder of the relentless passage of time. Yet, they pressed on, refusing to bow to the creeping despair.

In the quiet moments, when the Void's chaos was temporarily held at bay, their thoughts drifted back to their homes - the rolling golden plains of Piltover, the tranquil beauty of Ionia, the vast oceans of the Marai, and the ancient runes of Ryze's sanctuary. Homes and people that needed protecting, a mission that demanded completion.

As the unseen sun of the Void sunk below an imaginary horizon, a feeling of unity bonded them, despite the vast distances separating them. They were a team, their spirits intertwined, their goals aligned. The Void could play tricks on their senses, it could scatter them, it could whisper promises of despair, but it couldn't shatter their resolve.

The race against time was on, and they were determined to win. They were champions, and they would endure, for their friends, for their homes, and for Runeterra. The Void was their battlefield, and they were the soldiers. The clock was ticking, but so were their hearts, each beat a declaration of their indomitable will to reunite and conquer.

A Reunion and Revelation

As the alien sun rose once more, illuminating the grotesque Void landscape, a light flickered in the distance. Twisted Fate, his hat tipped low, squinted at the glow. A card twirled in his hand as he smirked, a glint of hope in his eyes. "Well, now," he drawled. "Looks like the lady luck's finally smilin' my way."

Ahri, her fox ears perked, detected a subtle change in the thrum of the Void. Her orb pulsed, reacting to a familiar energy. She sprinted towards the source, her nine tails leaving a trail of ethereal light in her wake.

Nami, her eyes shining with determination, wielded her staff, summoning a surge of magical energy that propelled her across the bizarre terrain. Her heart beat in rhythm with the tidecaller's pulse, guiding her to her friends.

Ryze, his runes radiating a bright blue hue, moved forward, undeterred by the vast expanse. The arcane energy within him resonated, a beacon calling out to the others.

In the heart of the Void, they converged. Their reunion was marked with quick nods and shared smiles, a testament to their bond. Despite their grim situation, the relief was palpable. The essence of their friendship, their unity, remained unscathed amidst the alien desolation.

Ryze, the Rune Mage, broke the silence, "We've lost time, but not hope." His eyes flicked to each of them, a silent nod of appreciation before he turned his gaze to the peculiar structure at the center of their meeting point.

A towering monolith of Void crystals stood before them, pulsating with a strange energy. As they approached, the energy swelled, reacting to their presence. It was then that Ahri's orb began to glow, a bright light that matched the monolith's pulsations.

"We're meant to be here," Ahri said, her voice carrying a note of certainty. With cautious steps, she moved closer to the monolith. Her orb floated towards the surface of the structure, the two sources of energy meeting in a radiant burst of light.

What followed was a cascade of images and sensations, an echo from the distant past. They saw the Void's creation, not as an act of chaos, but as a result of cosmic equilibrium. They saw the Void's purpose, not as a devouring entity, but as a mirror, reflecting and absorbing the excess of creation. And they saw its corruption, a tragic fall from balance to chaos.

As the visions subsided, the champions stood in silence, each processing the revelation. The Void, their enemy, was a victim itself, a distorted reflection of the cosmos.

With this new understanding, their mission became clearer. They were not just fighting to protect their world, but to restore balance to a fallen entity.

Confronting the Voidborn

In the alien world of the Void, there were few constants. The landscape shifted erratically, grotesque creatures lurked in the shadows, and time seemed to bend and warp in disconcerting ways. But amidst the chaos, the champions of Runeterra found steadiness in their shared determination.

Their recent discovery had given their mission a new dimension, casting the Void and its terrifying entities in a new light. It was no longer just about survival, but about understanding, perhaps even aiding this twisted realm. But theories and revelations needed to be tested, and the champions knew they had to confront one of the Voidborn to validate their suspicions.

A formidable challenge stood in their path. Vel'Koz, the Eye of the Void, a creature of pure malice and destructive curiosity. The Voidborn entity hovered above the ground, its single monstrous eye scanning the surroundings, radiating with a disquieting light.

"Well, aren't you a sight for sore eyes," Twisted Fate quipped, eyes locked with the Voidborn entity. His fingers danced over the deck of cards in his hand, ready to draw at a moment's notice.

Ahri stepped forward, her orb glowing brightly. "We're not here to fight you, Vel'Koz. We want to understand." Her voice echoed across the abyss, steady yet brimming with a sincere plea.

The Voidborn entity's attention shifted to Ahri, its eye narrowing as it studied her. "Understand? An intriguing proposition." The words echoed in their minds, the voice unsettling and cold.

Ryze, holding his scroll tightly, moved to stand by Ahri. His eyes were stern, his tone firm. "We've seen the past, the truth of the Void. We know there's more to you than just destruction."

Vel'Koz paused, its monstrous eye flickering as it processed the words. The champions held their breath, their weapons ready but their intentions clear. This was a diplomatic mission as much as it was a battle.

Then, without warning, Vel'Koz's eye flared with energy, and a barrage of Void energy rained down upon them. They scattered, employing their powers to defend themselves.

"Guess talkin' didn't pan out, eh?" Twisted Fate yelled, dodging a laser blast. But Ahri shook her head, her eyes on Vel'Koz.

"No, this is a test," she shouted back, her voice clear over the chaos. "He's testing our resolve!"

United in purpose and stronger than ever, the champions of Runeterra faced the onslaught. The battle raged, a dance of abilities and strategies, of magic and might. It was gruelling, it was arduous, but beneath the surface, it was a conversation, a plea for understanding.

With a final combined assault, they managed to halt Vel'Koz's attack. The Voidborn entity hovered, its eye pulsating weakly. There was a long pause before it spoke again, "You... are different. You seek not to destroy, but to balance."

As the words resonated, the champions shared a look of triumphant affirmation. Their theory had been confirmed. Now, they just needed to figure out how to restore the balance. Their journey in the Void was far from over, but they were one step closer to achieving their goal. They were not just champions of Runeterra anymore, but champions for the Void. And together, they would bring balance back to the cosmos.

The Void's Origin

In the aftermath of their confrontation with Vel'Koz, the champions of Runeterra found themselves awash with a mixture of relief and anticipation. Their gamble had paid off, their theory validated. The Void wasn't solely a realm of destruction; it held a semblance of balance, a balance they hoped to restore. The first part of their mission was completed. Now they had to unravel the Void's origin.

"Did ya'll hear what Vel'Koz said?" Twisted Fate asked, looking around at his companions as he shuffled his deck of cards. "About us being different."

Ryze nodded, his brows furrowing in thought. "Yes. And it's what he didn't say that's equally telling. He mentioned balance, not destruction. There's a structure to the Void, a purpose we need to understand."

"I believe the spirits can help with that," Ahri said. She closed her eyes and began to meditate, the nine tails swirling around her like a spectral shield. Her spiritual energy reached out, navigating through the swirling chaos of the Void.

As Ahri communed with the spirits, the champions found themselves immersed in a spectral projection of the past. They saw an advanced civilization, beings of celestial energy that twinkled like stars. They were the Ascended, the progenitors of the Void, who had created it as a space of balance, a realm to contain and neutralize the cosmic threats that endangered their reality.

But with time, the Void had evolved, the balance had tilted, birthing the Voidborn that now threatened their existence.

As the projection faded, the champions were left in stunned silence. The Void, their enemy, was a creation of the very beings they had revered as protectors of their world.

"So, our ancestors messed up and now we've to clean it up," Nami summarised, her usually jovial face solemn. "Feels a bit like a fish out of water, doesn't it?"

Ryze let out a dry chuckle. "Yes, I suppose it does. But it also gives us an edge. We now understand the Void's purpose."

Twisted Fate slid his hat off, running a hand through his hair. "So, we're here to restore balance, not just fight. Ain't that a twist?"

Ahri nodded, her eyes reflecting the spectral lights of the Void. "Yes. We're here to mend what was broken. We are the Champions of Runeterra, the bearers of balance. It's time we live up to that title."

A Universe of Chaos

As the revelation of the Ascended and the origins of the Void sank in, the champions found themselves cast adrift in a sea of new possibilities and implications. The world as they knew it, the realms and dimensions they had mapped and studied, all paled in comparison to the grand scale of cosmic events they were now embroiled in.

A silence settled over them, a contemplative hush that echoed through the otherworldly landscape of the Void. The eerie calm felt strange yet oddly fitting after the earth-shattering revelation.

Ryze, ever the scholar, was the first to break the silence. He began pacing, his arcane tattoos faintly glowing as he articulated his thoughts. "This changes everything," he said. "Our understanding of the cosmos, of our reality. If the Ascended could create a realm like the Void, what else is out there that we don't know?"

"The stars are more than just lights in the night sky," Nami mused, staring up at the strange constellations of the Void. "They're other worlds, other realities."

Twisted Fate, leaning against a crystalline formation, scoffed lightly. "And here I thought my world was just Runeterra and a couple of realms to pull my cards from. Turns out we're all just a tiny speck in a whole cosmos of chaos."

"That's quite the poetic take, Twisted Fate," Ahri commented with a playful smile. Yet, her eyes held a glimmer of apprehension. "But you're right. It's...overwhelming, to say the least."

The champions sat in contemplative silence, the weight of their discoveries pressing down on them. Yet, amid the shock and awe, there was a spark of excitement, a stirring of wonder. They were venturing into the unknown, uncovering cosmic secrets that could redefine their understanding of existence.

"It is a lot to take in," Ryze conceded. "But remember, we're not just passive observers. We are champions, chosen for a reason. Our actions, our choices...they shape our world, our universe."

Nami nodded, her gaze firm. "You're right, Ryze. The universe may be vast and chaotic, but we're part of it. And we'll fight to protect our part, no matter what."

"Couldn't have said it better myself, Tidecaller," Twisted Fate tipped his hat to Nami. "Guess it's time we get back to it. After all, we've got a cosmos to save."

With their resolve reaffirmed, the champions of Runeterra pressed on, carrying the weight of their newfound knowledge. They knew the road ahead would be fraught with danger, but they were ready to face whatever the Void, and the cosmos, had in store for them.

A Hope in Desolation

The vast and hostile expanse of the Void stretched before them, a daunting and seemingly insurmountable challenge. The champions of Runeterra, however, were no strangers to adversity. Amid the desolation, they clung fiercely to a sliver of hope that could perhaps turn the tide in their favor.

Kassadin, ever the experienced Voidwalker, pointed out the subtle patterns in the swirling abyss around them. "You see those energy currents? They dictate the flow of the Void, its growth and expansion. If we could disrupt those..."

"Like rerouting a river?" Twisted Fate suggested, his brow furrowed in thought.

Ryze nodded slowly, studying the currents with newfound interest. "Indeed, it's not entirely different. Although, the arcane laws governing the Void might be far more complex and unpredictable. But in theory..."

"In theory," Ahri interjected, her nine tails dancing anxiously behind her, "we could potentially slow the Void's growth, give Runeterra more time?"

"Time to prepare, to gather forces and fortify defenses," Nami added, her usually soft gaze hardening with determination.

Silence fell over the group as they contemplated the daunting task ahead. Each champion was lost in their thoughts, the weight of their responsibility settling heavily on their shoulders.

Finally, Twisted Fate broke the silence with a smirk, "Well, what are we waiting for then? Let's get to work."

The champions delved deeper into the mysterious energy currents, their minds occupied with complex calculations and strategies. Every move had to be made with precision, every action with careful consideration.

While they set to work, the Void seemed almost still around them, as if the monstrous realm itself was holding its breath. There was a spark of hope amid the desolation, a faint beacon of light in the heart of darkness.

Through their tireless efforts, the champions were not just observers in a cosmic event but active participants, pitting their skills, intellect, and sheer determination against a seemingly omnipotent force. And for the first time in their challenging journey, the Void felt less like an unconquerable enemy and more like a puzzle to be solved.

As the sun set over another day in the Void, painting the strange landscape in surreal hues, the champions of Runeterra continued their work. United in purpose and spurred on by hope, they delved deeper into the complexities of the Void, determined to protect their home from the looming threat.

Despite the despair around them, they clung fiercely to that glimmer of hope. In the chilling vastness of the Void, it was their most potent weapon.

Chapter 25: "The Final Stand" - The once familiar champions stood under the ethereal glow of the Void's pulsating heart, their expressions grave. This was it - the culmination of all their trials, their hopes, their fears. The silence was thick, only broken by the odd, unnerving sounds of the Void.

"It all comes down to this," Twisted Fate murmured, shuffling his cards nervously, the familiar motion a small comfort amid the swirling chaos around them.

Nami nodded, her grip on her staff tightening. The cool, luminous sphere at its end reflected in her determined eyes. "The current has led us here. We must not falter now."

Ahri flicked her ears, her tails flickering like nine ghostly flames. She stared at the Void's core, a storm of emotions swirling within her. "We will prevail. We must," she declared, her voice steady despite the chill creeping up her spine.

Ryze, the old Rune Mage, was quiet. His gaze was set on the swirling vortex of Void energy, the ancient runes on his arms glowing with anticipation. The power he commanded was immense, but so was the task ahead of them.

Kassadin stood slightly apart from the rest, his gaze distant. The Voidwalker had a personal vendetta against the Void, a personal score to settle. But right then, the fate of all Runeterra was in their hands, and he knew the weight of their responsibility.

"Alright, let's go over the plan one more time," he said, turning to the rest of the team.

Ryze stepped forward, laying out the map they had drawn of the Void's energy currents. "We need to channel our energy into these points," he pointed, tracing the paths on the map, "to disrupt the Void's growth."

"And this is where we make our stand," Twisted Fate added, pointing at the heart of the Void. "If we can manage to reroute the Void's energy currents and deal a blow to its heart at the same time, we might just have a chance."

The plan was risky, teetering on the edge of impossible, but they had no other choice. Each champion nodded, understanding the gravity of the situation. They were ready to fight, ready to defend their world.

With a collective breath, they stepped forward, ready to face the challenge head-on. They worked in tandem, each contributing their unique skills to the intricate task. Twisted Fate's cards whirred through the air, Nami's staff pulsed with power, Ahri's orbs danced around her, and Ryze's runes glowed brighter than ever.

All the while, Kassadin led the charge, his Void energy intertwining with the destructive force they sought to control. It was a dance of control and chaos, the champions' resolute spirits against the untamed wilderness of the Void.

Despite the odds, the champions of Runeterra stood strong, their determination undying. They had ventured into the heart of the enemy territory, faced unimaginable horrors, and now, they took their final stand.

As they braced themselves for the confrontation, one thing was clear: they would fight until the very end. For Runeterra. For home.

Victory at a Cost

Beneath the Void's swirling nebula, the champions stood resolute. The eldritch landscape, once a source of unease, had become their battlefield, a testament to their resilience and determination. They looked towards the heart of the Void, a swirling mass of cosmic energy, the epicenter of the chaos. Their gazes held the spark of resolve, glinting under the strange ethereal light.

"Are we ready?" Ryze asked, his voice stern yet resonant with the faint trace of concern. He glanced towards his companions, his gaze lingering on each one. From Twisted Fate, shuffling his cards nervously yet maintaining his nonchalant demeanor, to Nami, her eyes glinting with steely determination, each one mirrored his sentiment.

"We're as ready as we'll ever be," Nami responded, gripping her staff. A faint luminescence pulsed from the moonstone nestled at its crest.

Ahri's nine tails twitched in anticipation, her orbs of spirit energy orbiting her, reflecting her focused state. "Let's end this," she added.

There was a sense of finality to her words, hanging in the air like an unspoken oath. They had journeyed through the Void, confronted its horrors, and lived to tell the tale. Now, all that remained was to act on the plan that had been born of countless discussions, strategy sessions, and the revelations from the Void itself.

With a shared nod, they sprang into action. Ryze, with his arcane mastery, began weaving a complex glyph in the air. Ahri focused her spiritual energy, her magic mingling with the ever-shifting energies of the Void. Nami raised her staff, summoning a surge of cosmic waters that reflected the strange, nebulous light around them. Twisted Fate threw his cards into the swirling winds, each card charged with powerful magic.

They acted in perfect unison, their actions a testament to their shared experiences and unwavering trust in one another. Their combined magic reached out, intertwining with the volatile energies of the Void's heart.

Then, with a final, combined cry, they released their magic.

The world around them seemed to hold its breath as a brilliant light exploded from the heart of the Void, illuminating the abyss with its otherworldly glow. The energy surged, a wave of cosmic magic that swept across the void-touched landscape.

The Void trembled, quaking under the onslaught of the champions' combined power. It resisted, its void-born creatures howling as they were swept up in the chaos. But the champions held their ground, their determination unyielding.

Finally, after an eternity that lasted but moments, the light subsided. The heart of the Void pulsed weakly, its power visibly diminished.

The champions stood, panting and visibly drained, but triumphant. They had achieved what many would have considered impossible. They had confronted the Void and won.

But victory came at a cost. As the glow of triumph faded, Twisted Fate collapsed, the exertion proving too much for him. Ahri rushed to his side, her eyes wide with panic.

"No...no!" she cried. "Stay with us!"

As Nami and Ryze hurried to join her, the grim reality of their victory set in. They had won, but not without sacrifice. And as they huddled around their fallen companion, their joy of victory was overshadowed by a profound sorrow.

The Void may have been defeated, but the scars of their journey would remain, a painful reminder of the price of their victory. Their journey was over, but it was a conclusion tinted with the bittersweet taste of loss.

In the echoing silence of the Void, beneath the twinkling alien stars, the champions mourned. Their victory chant was not a roar of triumph, but a solemn vow. A promise to remember the cost, to honor the sacrifice, and to stand together, always.

The Aftermath

The Void, once a riotous cacophony of alien energies and grotesque void-born creatures, now lay hushed. The residual echoes of their victory still vibrated in the air, the silence thick and palpable.

As Ahri cradled the unconscious Twisted Fate, the euphoria of their triumph was tempered by the grim reminder of their loss. Her gaze shifted from the motionless form of her comrade to the heart of the Void. Diminished and subdued, it pulsed weakly, a shadow of its former self.

Nami stood alongside her, her moonstone staff dimmed. In her eyes, a profound understanding had taken root. She had ventured into the Void, an emissary from the oceanic depths, and returned forever changed.

Ryze, the Rune Mage, his power spent, looked at his companions, his heart heavy with a cocktail of emotions - pride, relief, sorrow, and an overwhelming sense of responsibility.

As they stood in the aftermath of their victory, the enormity of their task loomed ahead. They had to return to Runeterra, to heal and to spread the word of what they had discovered.

"The journey back won't be easy," Ryze warned, breaking the silence. He looked at each of his companions in turn. "But we can't stay here. We must return to Runeterra."

"Twisted Fate needs help," Ahri added, her voice choked. The reality of their situation threatened to unravel the remnants of her composure.

"We won't abandon him," Nami said, her voice firm. "We face this together, as we always have."

As if to punctuate her sentiment, the heart of the Void pulsed again, casting long, ghastly shadows over the desolate landscape. It was a grim reminder that they were still in the heart of enemy territory.

Summoning the last dregs of their energy, the champions set to work. Using Ryze's knowledge of ancient magic, Ahri's spiritual energy, and Nami's command of water, they created a makeshift stretcher for Twisted Fate. They began their long, arduous trek, every step a testament to their resolve.

The journey was silent, save for the occasional growl of a distant void-born creature or the hum of alien energies. Despite their exhaustion and the haunting memories of their recent battle, their spirits remained undeterred. They found comfort in their shared silence, their shared ordeal serving as a bond that ran deeper than words could express.

As the champions began their journey back to Runeterra, their hearts carried the weight of their experiences. They were returning as harbingers of a hard-won victory, but also as bearers of a grave warning. Their world view had been irrevocably changed, their perception of reality expanded beyond the confines of their homeworld.

For now, their objective was to reach home, to heal, to regroup. They had won the battle, but the war against the Void was far from over.

With the image of the subdued heart of the Void etched in their memories, they trudged on, determined to face whatever awaited them in their world. They were ready to confront any challenge that stood in their path.

The Homecoming

The light of Runeterra greeted the champions with a warm embrace, the golden rays of dawn cascading over their weary forms as they emerged from the residual rift. Their senses, dulled by the endless monochrome of the Void, drank in the lush vibrancy of their home world.

Ahri was the first to break the silence. "It feels strange," she confessed, her voice a mere whisper carried on the wind. Her fox ears twitched, her tails swaying as she absorbed the familiar yet overwhelming stimuli of Runeterra.

Ryze nodded, his eyes surveying the familiar landscape with renewed appreciation. "It does," he agreed. "But it's good to be back."

Nami murmured an agreement, her attention divided between her companions and the unconscious form of Twisted Fate. Her heart ached for their friend, for the unspoken grief they all shared.

Their homecoming, albeit a welcome respite, was shadowed by the lingering spectre of their ordeals. They had returned victorious, yet scarred, their perspectives forever skewed by their experiences in the Void.

"We should inform the Council," Ryze finally voiced the thought that had been lurking in their minds. "They must be made aware of what we discovered."

A bitter laugh escaped Ahri. "And you think they will believe us, old man?" she asked, a glimmer of her usual teasing tone cutting through the sombreness.

"They must," Nami said firmly. "For the sake of Runeterra."

They had returned with a weighty responsibility, bearing revelations that could shake the very foundations of their world's understanding of the cosmos. They were heroes, yes, but they were also harbingers of grave news that needed to be shared, accepted, and acted upon.

In the days that followed, they each resumed their respective roles. Ryze, the Rune Mage, petitioned to speak before the Council of Summoners. Ahri, the Nine-Tailed Fox, found solace in the familiarity of the Ionian forests, her heart aching for the friend they'd left behind in the Void.

And Nami, the Tidecaller, ventured back to her oceanic home, her role as a messenger now carrying a more significant meaning. She had ventured beyond the ocean, beyond Runeterra, and had returned changed, imbued with a deeper understanding of their universe.

Their journey had taken them to the heart of the Void and back. They had stared into the abyss and returned with their spirits unbroken. But the journey was far from over.

As the sun set, painting the sky with hues of gold, orange, and purple, the champions stood united in spirit, ready to bear the weight of their discoveries. This was their homecoming, a moment of respite in their ongoing journey. And they knew, when the time came, they would face the future challenges together, as champions of Runeterra.

Lessons of the Void

In the tranquil forest of Ionia, Ahri stood at the edge of a cliff, overlooking the gentle roll of the sea. The sun was setting, casting long shadows that danced over the undergrowth, painting the leaves in hues of gold and crimson. For the first time since her return, the forest felt familiar, comforting.

Her hand traced the ancient markings on a nearby tree, each character a testament to a story that had long passed. Now she too had a story, one that was etched deep in her heart. Her tails swished thoughtfully, her ears perked as if expecting the Void's dissonant echo. But there was only the calming rustle of leaves, the distant call of birds returning to their nests.

"Lessons of the Void," Ahri murmured, her eyes reflecting the twilight. Her journey had taught her about strength, about courage, about sacrifice. It had shown her a glimpse of the cosmos' vast, unfathomable secrets. And yet, the most profound lesson she had gleaned was closer to home: the value of unity and friendship.

Across the realm, in the heart of the Blue Flame Isles, Ryze stood within the confines of his arcane sanctum. Runes floated around him, pulsating with potent energy. His eyes were focused, the weight of their journey manifest in his stoic countenance. But there was a spark of renewed determination in his gaze.

The Void had been a testament to the chaos of unchecked power, a chilling reminder of what could occur when magic was left to rampage unchecked. He, the Rune Mage, held the responsibility of safeguarding the World Runes. Their journey had only solidified his resolve, the lessons of the Void lending him the strength to carry his burden.

In the depths of the ocean, Nami swam gracefully amongst her Marai kin. She listened to the murmur of the currents, the whispers of the sea echoing the songs of her people. The Void had been devoid of such melodies, a silent desolation that had felt heavier than the deepest sea.

Her role as the Tidecaller had always been about communication, about carrying messages from the depths to the surface. Now, her journey had granted her a new message, a new lesson. The Void had taught her about the resilience of life, the persistent spark of hope amidst desolation. It was a lesson she would carry with her, a constant reminder that no matter the depth of the darkness, there would always be a beacon of hope.

The Void had been a journey of trials and revelations, a confrontation with an alien realm that had tested their resolve. Yet, as each champion reflected upon their experiences, they realised that the true lessons of the Void were not of alien entities or cosmic chaos.

Instead, they were lessons of unity, of resolve, of hope. Lessons that were deeply personal, yet universally poignant. Lessons that would forever echo in their hearts, resonating with their every step as they continued their roles as champions of Runeterra.

The Enigma Unveiled

In the bustling heart of Piltover, Caitlyn stared down at a blueprint sprawled across her desk. The diagrams were intricate, the calculations precise. Yet her thoughts were not on her latest invention, but rather on the lingering echoes of their recent journey. She traced a hand over the diagrams, her mind travelling back to the pulsating heart of the Void.

Her companions, champions all, had returned to their respective corners of Runeterra, each bearing the weight of their journey. There had been victory, yes, but it had come with a sobering revelation. The Void was not merely a cosmic aberration; it was an entity in itself, with a potential for evolution that was as unsettling as it was unpredictable.

A knock at the door startled her out of her reverie. It was Vi, her trusted friend and partner. "Caught up in your thoughts again?" Vi asked, her eyes reflecting a shared understanding. They had faced the trials of the Void together, their bond solidified in the face of cosmic adversity.

"Always," Caitlyn replied with a grim smile. "Remember what Ryze said? The Void... it's not over. It's merely dormant, waiting for its next cycle."

Vi's face hardened, her resolve evident. "We handled it once. We'll do it again. No matter what the Void evolves into, we'll be ready."

Elsewhere in Ionia, Ahri shared a similar discussion with Karma, the serene leader deeply disturbed by Ahri's recount of their encounter with the Void. "The balance of the world has been shifted," Karma murmured, her eyes darkened with concern.

"We must prepare," Ahri agreed, her tails twitching uneasily. "The Void we confronted was formidable. But what it will become... it's an enigma we need to unravel."

In the depths of the Shadow Isles, Yorick stood alone, watching the spectral mists dance before him. His mind was occupied with the whispers of the Void, the ghostly echoes resonating with his own spectral existence. His grip tightened around the edge of his shovel. The Void had been quelled, but it was far from vanquished.

Across Runeterra, the heroes braced themselves, aware of the brewing storm. They had uncovered the mysteries of the Void, only to reveal an enigma wrapped within. The Void was evolving, transforming into something more potent, more complex.

The trials of their journey had left an indelible mark on each of them. There was no return to the bliss of ignorance, to the comfort of oblivion. The enigma had been unveiled, and with it came the harsh light of reality. The Void was no longer a distant menace, it was an inevitable threat looming in Runeterra's future.

As they prepared for the trials to come, they took solace in one unshakeable truth. They were champions, defenders of Runeterra, forged in the crucible of the Void. They had faced the cosmic abyss and emerged victorious.

And when the time came, they would stand together once more, ready to confront whatever the Void became. For the sake of Runeterra, for the sake of their world, they would face the enigma unveiled and, once again, emerge victorious.

PART 3
The Tournament

Introduction

The sun was setting on Runeterra, casting long shadows over the landscape. The City of Progress, Piltover, glowed with the light of a thousand arc lamps, while the undercity of Zaun lay shrouded in smog and twilight. From the lofty heights of Mount Targon to the murky depths of the Shadow Isles, a curious hush fell upon the land.

A sudden gust of wind swirled through the regions, carrying with it a proclamation. Encrypted in magic and wrapped in mystery, it promised a grand tournament, a competition between champions from all across the realm.

In the frost-rimed wilds of the Freljord, the message appeared as swirling snowflakes to Ashe, the Frost Archer. Within the Ionian Monastery, it was an mysterious whisper of wind around Zed, the Master of Shadows. The message danced as sparks on the tips of Demacian soldier Garen's sword, the incandescent embers of a magical flame in the hands of Lux, and as shifting shadows beneath the deathly lantern of Thresh, the Chain Warden.

In the heart of Piltover, the proclamation transformed into a cryptic pattern in the machinery tinkered by Ezreal, the Prodigal Explorer. In the chaotic depths of Zaun, it was a rhythmic rattle of bullets in the cannon of Jinx, the Loose Cannon. And in the Grand Duelist's training ground, Fiora felt an unusual chill running down her rapier's edge.

The announcement was the same, yet uniquely tailored to each champion: an invitation to participate in a grand tournament, a test of power, strategy, and spirit. The prize? A reward beyond their wildest dreams, one that held the potential to change not just their fate, but the course of Runeterra itself.

As intriguing as the promise of the prize was the mystery of the one who promised it. The Tournament Master, a figure unknown and unseen, whose intentions were as mysterious as the magic that brought the message to the champions.

Who was this Tournament Master? What did they truly seek? The curiosity was as alluring as the grandeur of the prize. Drawn by the mystery and the thrill of competition, the chosen champions accepted the invitation, ready to pit their strength and wits against each other.

They would soon learn that this was more than a game; it was a crucible that would test their limits and force them to confront their deepest fears. The future of Runeterra hung in the balance, and the journey that lay ahead was fraught with peril, mystery, and intrigue.

The sun dipped beneath the horizon, its last rays disappearing into the darkness. The game was set, the players were chosen, and as the moon rose, casting a silver glow over the realm, the grandest spectacle Runeterra had ever seen was about to unfold.

The Challenge

In the heart of Demacia's grand palace, a mysterious figure emerged, silhouetted by the imposing structure's shadow. The figure, shrouded in an elegant cloak, moved with an undeniable air of authority that commanded the attention of everyone present. This was the Tournament Master, and he bore a message for all of Runeterra.

"My Champions of Runeterra," his voice rang out, amplified by some unknown magic to echo throughout the palace halls and beyond. "I propose a challenge, a tournament unlike any you have seen before. For the victor, a prize of unimaginable power and wisdom."

The assembled champions exchanged curious looks, intrigue sparked in their eyes. Ashe, the Frost Archer from Freljord, was the first to break the silence, her voice cool as the winter's wind. "And who are you to call us to a challenge? You, shrouded in mystery, dare to command the attention of Runeterra's champions?"

The Tournament Master chuckled, a sound that rang with an almost unsettling joy. "I am but a humble servant of competition, a catalyst for your evolution and growth. I am the Tournament Master."

Thresh, the Chain Warden from the Shadow Isles, rumbled a laugh from beneath his spectral cowl. "A fine title, but how do we know this isn't a trap? What guarantee do we have?"

"Ah, the Warden questions my intentions, as he should. But fear not, my spectral friend. I desire nothing more than to see the best of you brought to light in the arena," the Tournament Master responded.

Fiora, the Grand Duelist of Demacia, stepped forward, her gaze fixed on the puzzling figure. "You ask us to compete for a prize we know nothing about. Reveal its nature to us."

The Tournament Master simply raised a gloved hand, a cryptic smile playing on his lips. "All in due time, Lady Laurent. For now, suffice to say that the prize is something worth your trials and efforts."

A murmur spread through the crowd of champions. The Tournament Master's challenge had been laid down. Whether driven by curiosity, ambition, or a desire for the unknown prize, the champions of Runeterra felt the thrill of the upcoming challenge.

"Prepare yourselves, Champions," the Tournament Master declared, a hint of anticipation seeping into his voice. "The tournament begins in three days. May the odds be ever in your favor."

With those final words, the figure disappeared as mysteriously as he had arrived, leaving behind a flurry of questions, anticipation, and a burning desire for victory. The tournament was now the talk of Runeterra, and the champions, whether they accepted the challenge or not, knew that their world was on the brink of something monumental.

The Selection

In the days following the Tournament Master's announcement, speculation ran wild across Runeterra. Champions debated, argued, and pondered over the upcoming competition. It was on the third day, at the break of dawn, that the Tournament Master reappeared.

His sudden presence in the grand hall of Demacia's palace commanded silence. He raised a gloved hand, and eight envelopes, each emblazoned with a unique crest, floated into the air, surrounded by an ethereal glow.

"The eight chosen for this tournament," he began, his voice echoing throughout the hall, "have been selected not only for their strength and prowess but also for their wisdom, courage, and heart."

The first envelope, bearing the emblem of the Frost Archer, glided to Ashe. Her eyes widened slightly, but she accepted it with a determined nod.

The second, marked with the emblem of the Master of Shadows, drifted towards Zed. He caught the envelope with a swift movement, a shadowy smirk on his face.

Fiora, Garen, and Lux, representing the pride and strength of Demacia, received the third, fourth, and fifth envelopes, their expressions a mixture of surprise and determination.

Ezreal, the Prodigal Explorer, barely looked up from an ancient map to catch the sixth envelope. "Hmm, interesting development," he mumbled, studying the crest on the envelope before tucking it safely in his pocket.

Thresh, the Chain Warden, watched the seventh envelope approach him, his lantern illuminating the emblem. A dark laugh echoed around him as he clasped it in his spectral hand.

Finally, the eighth envelope, bearing the symbol of the Loose Cannon, whizzed towards Jinx. She plucked it from the air, her manic grin growing wider.

"The eight of you will compete in the grand tournament," the Tournament Master continued, his gaze sweeping over the selected champions. "I encourage you to prepare yourselves mentally, emotionally, and physically. This is not just a test of power, but of your very essence."

With that, he disappeared again, leaving the chosen champions to digest this revelation. Whispers filled the air, eyes darted towards the selected, and a flurry of emotions rippled through the crowd. The champions began to prepare themselves, the stakes of the mysterious tournament now all too real.

"A tournament, huh?" Jinx giggled, twirling the envelope around her finger. "Sounds like fun."

The First Battle

The entire realm of Runeterra was abuzz with excitement as the day of the first duel arrived. The Tournament Master had chosen a grand arena suspended over a churning sea, where the sound of crashing waves added an extra layer of drama to the impending battle. The crowd waited with bated breath as Ashe, the Frost Archer, and Zed, the Master of Shadows, stepped onto the field.

Ashe, with her blue-white hair cascading over her fur-lined cloak, had a serene yet focused demeanor. She carried her bow, Avarosa's legacy, with a sense of honor and determination. Her gaze was ice, her resolve unshaken.

Across the field, Zed stood as a stark contrast. Shrouded in an aura of shadowy energy, his masked figure radiated an intense, menacing energy. His blades, extensions of his will, gleamed ominously under the arena's magical lights.

As they faced each other, the Tournament Master's voice boomed over the arena, "Let the first battle begin!"

With the echo of the words still lingering, Ashe swiftly notched an arrow, her fingers gliding smoothly over the fletching. But Zed was faster. With a flourish of his hand, he disappeared into a puff of shadows.

Ashe spun around, launching a volley of arrows towards the shimmering shadowy figure reappearing behind her. The arrows pierced through the shadows, but Zed had already moved, his form flickering from one shadow to another.

"Predictable, Frost Archer," Zed mocked, his voice coming from all directions as he manipulated the shadows.

"I prefer dependable," Ashe retorted, her voice steady as she launched an enchanted arrow into the sky.

Zed emerged from the shadows, charging towards her, blades ready. Just as he was about to strike, Ashe's enchanted arrow exploded in a blinding storm of ice above them. The arena was enveloped in a blizzard, reducing visibility to near zero.

Zed, disoriented by the sudden change in environment, barely had time to react as Ashe materialized from the snow, her arrow aimed straight at him. He managed to deflect the arrow with his blades, but the momentum forced him back, causing him to stumble.

Taking advantage of his confusion, Ashe swiftly released a flurry of arrows. Zed, still regaining his footing, could not dodge in time. An arrow struck his shoulder, and he was thrown off balance. Before he could recover, another arrow pinned his cloak to the ground.

"Dependable indeed," Ashe said, walking over to him with confident strides. Zed, trapped under Ashe's precision, could only offer a grudging nod of respect.

As the blizzard subsided and the arena returned to its normal state, the crowd erupted in cheers. The first battle of the tournament had set the tone - this was not just about raw power, but strategy, skill, and the champions' very essence.

Mystery Unveiled

In the aftermath of the first exhilarating duel, a sense of anticipation lingered in the air. The participants retired to their quarters, their minds busy replaying the events and devising strategies for their upcoming matches. However, Ezreal, the Prodigal Explorer, and Lux, the Lady of Luminosity, found their curiosity piqued by something else: the mysterious Tournament Master.

Ezreal, with his unkempt golden hair and his trademark smirk, met Lux in the grand library within the tournament's castle. Lux, her golden locks tied up in a high ponytail, and her ever-present staff by her side, looked ready for a different kind of investigation.

"So," Ezreal started, leaning against a bookcase, his gauntlet glinting in the candlelight, "The Tournament Master. Mysterious, don't you think?"

Lux raised an eyebrow, her blue eyes sparkling with intrigue. "I thought you'd be more excited about the prospect of winning the tournament."

"I am," he replied, grinning, "But where's the fun without a side adventure? Besides, don't you want to know who's behind all this?"

Lux considered for a moment, then nodded. "Alright. Let's start investigating."

The two began pouring over ancient texts, maps, and magical artifacts, searching for any clues that could hint at the Tournament Master's identity. Hours passed, punctuated by hushed discussions and the rustling of parchment.

Finally, Lux discovered something. "Ezreal," she whispered, her voice filled with excitement. "Look at this."

She pointed to an old legend about a grand tournament held centuries ago, overseen by a mysterious entity known as the "Master of Tournaments." The description was vague, but certain parallels were impossible to ignore.

"Do you think our Tournament Master could be the same person?" Lux asked, her eyes wide with anticipation.

Ezreal, reading over her shoulder, nodded slowly. "It's possible. If it is, then we're dealing with a being who's centuries old. But why now? Why hold this tournament in this era?"

Before Lux could respond, a shadow fell over the library's entrance. They both turned to see a hooded figure, the air around them shimmering with a familiar energy.

"The curiosity of champions," the figure's voice echoed through the room, sounding eerily like the Tournament Master. "How very interesting."

As the figure vanished, leaving Ezreal and Lux in stunned silence, it became clear that their investigation had just taken a thrilling turn. The mystery of the Tournament Master was far from being solved, and their journey to the truth was just beginning.

Test of Skill

As the sun dipped below the horizon, painting the sky with vibrant hues of orange and purple, the tournament grounds buzzed with nervous energy. An eclectic mix of people from all across Runeterra filled the stands, their faces alight with anticipation. Among them were traders from Piltover, shamans from the Freljord, and soldiers from Demacia, their differences momentarily forgotten in the shared excitement of the upcoming duel.

Standing at one end of the massive sand-filled arena was Fiora, the Grand Duelist of Demacia, her slender figure poised with an air of confidence. Clad in her intricate battle gear, her hand was clasped around her gleaming rapier, the blade appearing as an extension of her own will. Her steely eyes were focused on one point alone: her opponent.

On the other side of the battlefield stood Garen, the Might of Demacia, a stalwart symbol of his homeland's values. A mountain of a man, he carried his hefty broadsword with an ease that spoke volumes about his strength. Dressed in armor that shimmered under the torchlight, he was the embodiment of Demacian fortitude and pride.

"Fiora," Garen called across the arena, his deep voice reverberating through the silent crowd. His eyes met Fiora's, reflecting a mutual understanding. "I promise to give this fight everything I have."

A smirk played on Fiora's lips, her grip tightening around her rapier. "And I expect nothing less, Garen."

As the final word left her lips, a horn blasted through the arena, signalling the start of the duel. With a thunderous cheer from the crowd, Garen charged forward, his broadsword raised for a devastating strike. But Fiora was quick, her nimble form sidestepping his attack, her rapier glinting menacingly under the torchlight.

Their battle raged on, turning into a beautiful, deadly dance. Garen's brute strength and raw power clashed against Fiora's finesse and precise technique. With each strike and parry, the crowd gasped, the champions' contrasting styles adding to the spectacle.

But despite Garen's relentless onslaught, Fiora was a whirlwind of motion. Her rapier was a blur, each precise thrust and slice a testament to her unparalleled skill. And when Garen launched a powerful attack that shook the arena, Fiora's agility saw her evade it with grace, her taunting reply making Garen grit his teeth in determination.

Their exchange of blows went on, the tension mounting with each passing second. Sweat trickled down their faces, their breaths becoming labored, but neither champion was willing to concede. It was a testament to their will, their determination, and above all, their unparalleled skill.

The deciding moment came when Fiora saw an opening, a small lapse in Garen's otherwise sturdy defense. With a swift feint and lunge, she struck, her rapier hitting its mark, and Garen fell to his knees in concession.

The crowd went silent for a moment, then erupted in an explosion of cheers and applause. Fiora stood victorious, her chest heaving as she looked down at her defeated opponent. And Garen, despite his loss, managed to give Fiora a nod of respect, acknowledging her superior skill.

"Well fought, Fiora," he managed, his voice husky with exertion.

Fiora, looking at Garen, allowed a small smile to grace her lips. "And you as well, Garen. You were a worthy opponent."

As the cheers of the crowd filled the night, ringing off the stone walls of the arena, the spotlight moved away from the victorious Fiora and the

Shadow and Light

In the heart of the arena, under the fading twilight, Lux, the Lady of Luminosity, stood resolute and bright against the encroaching darkness. She held her ornate staff aloft, the radiant crystal at its peak shimmering in an ethereal glow that cast long shadows across the battlefield. Her eyes, a mirror of the firmament above, were locked on the spectral figure hovering at the other end of the field.

Thresh, the Chain Warden, was a horrifying contrast to Lux's luminosity. A spectral being of shadow and torment, he lurked at the edge of darkness, his glowing eyes and the spectral lantern he carried the only features visible in his ghastly silhouette. The chilling rattle of his chains echoed ominously, bouncing off the stone walls of the arena and chilling the collective spine of the spectators.

"Thresh," Lux's voice rang out across the arena, clear as a bell in the silence of anticipation. Her staff shone brighter as she spoke, the aura around it pulsating in rhythm with her words. "You may use your chains to control, but I fight for freedom."

Thresh's response was a haunting laugh that echoed around the grounds, sending a ripple of unease through the crowd. "And how do you intend to fight me, Lady of Luminosity? With your light? Your hope?"

The crowd held its breath as Thresh, without waiting for her reply, lunged towards Lux, his chains whirling menacingly in the air. Lux reacted quickly, her staff glowing brighter as a beam of concentrated light shot forth, slicing through the darkness and stopping Thresh's advance.

Their battle turned into a mesmerizing dance of light and shadow. Thresh, with his dark chains and spectral skills, tried to entrap and overpower Lux. But Lux was unyielding. Each time his chains lashed out, she retaliated with bursts of light, her spells tearing through his onslaught and protecting her from his control.

Throughout their battle, Thresh's taunts echoed across the field. He tried to undermine Lux, to make her question her beliefs, her ideals. But Lux, with every dodge and counter-attack, proved her resolve. Her retorts to his jeers were filled with conviction, reaffirming her unwavering belief in her cause and herself.

As the fight raged on, Lux's resolve seemed to strengthen. Her every move was precise, her spells growing more powerful and blinding. And when Thresh launched what looked like a decisive attack, Lux held her ground. With a determined look in her eyes, she channeled her magic into her staff. A moment later, she unleashed it in a brilliant explosion of light.

The crowd shielded their eyes from the blinding light that engulfed the arena. And when it receded, they opened their eyes to see Lux standing in the middle of the arena, her staff still glowing brightly. Thresh lay defeated on the ground, his spectral form flickering weakly.

As Lux raised her staff high in victory, the crowd erupted into cheers. Her words, clear and resolute, echoed through the arena, a statement of her victory and a reaffirmation of her beliefs.

"The power of control you seek, Thresh," she declared, "will always be outshone by the power of choice!"

With her victory, Lux didn't just win a duel in the tournament, but also the symbolic battle of ideologies. The spectacle was a testament to her strength and belief, a triumph of freedom over control, of light over darkness.

The Maverick's Gambit

Ezreal stood at one end of the massive arena, his pulse quickening as he looked across the field at his opponent. Jinx, the Loose Cannon herself, grinned back at him, a gleam of mischief in her eyes that matched the dangerous glint of her massive rocket launcher, Fishbones.

"Ready to lose, pretty boy?" she called, her voice echoing across the expanse.

Ezreal's brow arched, his lips curling into a smirk. "Careful, Jinx," he replied, his hand on the handle of his gauntlet. "You're talking to the Prodigal Explorer here."

A deafening blast signaled the start of their battle. Ezreal dodged, skillfully evading the torrent of bullets that exploded from Pow-Pow, Jinx's minigun. His own attacks were swift and precise, magical energy bolts shooting from his gauntlet with calculated accuracy.

But Jinx was as unpredictable as ever. Her tactics seemed chaotic, with her switching between her weapons and laughing maniacally as she avoided his every shot with a dancer's grace.

Suddenly, Jinx paused, an uncharacteristic calm taking over her. "Time for some fun, Ezreal!" she said, her voice deceptively sweet. She began tinkering with her rocket launcher, adding what seemed to be an arcane crystal into the weapon. The crowd held its breath in anticipation.

Ezreal's eyes narrowed, realizing her unpredictable gambit. "Not on my watch, Jinx!" He aimed his gauntlet and fired a barrage of arcane energy, racing against time to stop her.

But Jinx's laughter rang out as a gigantic rocket shot out of Fishbones, soaring towards him. The rocket exploded before impact, releasing a shockwave of energy that knocked Ezreal off his feet.

As the dust settled, Jinx's wild laughter echoed through the stunned silence of the arena. Ezreal was on the ground, his gauntlet sparking with residual energy. The announcer declared, "Jinx, the winner!"

The crowd erupted, half in shock, half in awe, at the maverick's unexpected gambit. And all Ezreal could do as he lay on the ground was grin and shake his head.

"You're one crazy girl, Jinx," he muttered. But in the thrill of the tournament, he couldn't deny that it was battles like these that made everything exciting.

The Prize

In the waning sunlight that bathed the gargantuan arena, Ezreal stood at one end, the sand under his boots shifting uneasily. The breeze teased his blonde hair, carrying with it the anticipatory silence of the gathered crowd. On the opposite side, Jinx - the Loose Cannon - was a stark contrast, her maniacal grin spread wide, her eyes sparkling with mirth, and the ominous presence of her oversized rocket launcher, Fishbones, cradled in her arms.

"Ready to kiss the ground, golden boy?" Her voice ricocheted off the stone walls, a taunt wrapped in reckless glee.

Ezreal's lips curled into a smirk, his brows arched in amused disbelief. "You're barking up the wrong tree, Jinx," he countered, his fingers drumming a quick rhythm on his mystical gauntlet. "You should remember who you're dealing with."

A thunderous explosion marked the beginning of the contest. Ezreal was a blur, nimbly sidestepping the shower of bullets raining down from Pow-Pow, Jinx's high-powered minigun. His Mystic Shots, imbued with arcane energy and shot from his gauntlet, traced bright trajectories through the evening air, each one aimed with deadly precision.

Jinx, though, was a hurricane, her movements unpredictable, her methods as chaotic as they were effective. She bobbed and weaved, her laughter a haunting melody as she effortlessly dodged his assaults, all the while switching between her deadly arsenal of weapons.

Suddenly, the battlefield fell into an eerie quiet. Jinx was still, an unusual serenity replacing her usual frenzy. "Ready for a surprise, Ez?" Her voice was unnaturally sweet, a wolf hiding in sheep's clothing. With practiced ease, she began to modify Fishbones, slotting an arcane crystal into the weapon, her grin never faltering.

Ezreal's heart pounded against his ribcage, his instincts screaming at the impending threat. "Not today, Jinx!" His gauntlet glowed brighter as he prepared his next barrage, his eyes never leaving her.

But it was too late. With a triumphant cackle, Jinx unleashed a rocket of monstrous proportions. It cut through the air, the trail of its path etched in the collective memory of the crowd. The explosion was cataclysmic, the resultant shockwave knocking Ezreal off his feet.

The dust eventually settled, revealing a victorious Jinx and a grounded Ezreal, his gauntlet crackling with unfired energy. The crowd broke their silence, a tumultuous mix of shock and awe as they absorbed the outcome.

"Jinx, the winner!" The announcer's voice boomed.

Ezreal could only laugh, the taste of sand and defeat unfamiliar on his tongue. "You're something else, Jinx," he coughed out, but even in the face of defeat, he couldn't deny the thrill that the tournament offered. It was these unpredictable, high-stakes battles that made the entire ordeal worth it.

The Second Round

The atmosphere in the tournament grounds was thick with anticipation and anxiety as the second round was announced. The first round of battles had seen the fall of some and the rise of others, leaving four remaining champions – Ashe, Fiora, Lux and Jinx – in the contest.

Each champion found themselves grappling with their own doubts and fears. The stakes were high, not just for the mysterious prize, but also for their personal pride and honour.

In the common quarters, Ashe was seen honing her arrowheads, her forehead creased with concentration. She hadn't said much since her investigation with Zed. Her thoughts were elsewhere, on the symbol of the Void they had discovered.

Across the room, Fiora was deep in meditation. Her duel with Garen had been a testing one, and she was determined to win the next battle. Her reputation as the Grand Duelist was at stake.

Lux, on the other hand, was engrossed in her own dilemma. She had barely scraped through the first round against Thresh, and the thought of losing in the second was unsettling.

Jinx, however, seemed least bothered. She was humming to herself, tinkering with her rocket launcher, Fishbones, in her usual carefree manner.

Finally, the Tournament Master's voice boomed across the grounds, "Champions! It is time for the second round."

Ashe met Lux's gaze and gave her a nod. Lux returned the gesture, straightening her shoulders. Across them, Jinx gave Fiora a wide grin, which was met with a dignified nod. Despite their differences, they had grown to respect each other in their own way.

Each champion moved towards the tournament ground, their heart pounding in their chests. As the crowd cheered and the sun set, bathing the field in a golden glow, they couldn't shake off the feeling that the tournament was more than what it seemed.

But for now, they had a battle to win. For their pride, for their people, and for the mysterious prize that held unknown promises or dangers. With their weapons in hand and determination in their hearts, they stepped into the arena, ready to face the challenges of the second round.

The Reveal

Lux and Ezreal stood in the dimly lit library of the tournament grounds, their brows furrowed in deep concentration as they went through numerous books and scrolls, seeking any clue about the true identity of the Tournament Master. The dust-filled room was testament to the fact that it hadn't been visited in ages.

"Another dead end," Ezreal groaned, pushing away a book with an exasperated sigh. "These records are older than Zilean's hat, and still nothing!"

Lux, on the other hand, kept scanning through an old parchment. There was something about the Tournament Master that had made her suspicious since the very start. His confident demeanor and the concealed power she sensed from him; it was as if she had felt it somewhere before.

Suddenly, Lux gasped, causing Ezreal to startle and drop a scroll. "I found something!" she exclaimed, pointing at a portion of the parchment that was adorned with a symbol identical to the one on the Tournament Master's scepter.

"The seal of ancient Shuriman Royalty," Ezreal recognized, eyes widening in surprise. "But that doesn't make sense, the royal lineage..."

"They vanished millennia ago," Lux completed his sentence, her gaze serious. "But what if one of them survived? What if the Tournament Master is a surviving member?"

"Then his magical abilities make sense, the Shuriman royalty were powerful ascendants," Ezreal added, looking at Lux. "But the question remains, what does he aim to achieve from this tournament?"

Before they could further contemplate the implications of their discovery, a sudden cold voice echoed in the library, "Indeed, what does he aim to achieve?"

They turned around, only to find the Tournament Master standing at the entrance, an unreadable smile on his face. The room seemed to drop several degrees colder, a testament to his power and control. "Well done, Luxanna Crownguard, Ezreal... or should I say, the Prodigal Explorer."

The true identity of the Tournament Master was no longer a mystery. But with this revelation came an entirely new set of questions, ones that were far more dangerous and concerning.

Showdown of the Shadows

Beneath the ominous, purple-tinged skies of the Tournament grounds, a hushed stillness enveloped the audience. The impending clash between Zed, the Master of Shadows, and Fiora, the Grand Duelist, was the stuff of legends, a promised spectacle of lethal elegance and ingenious strategy that had everyone holding their breath.

The resonating clang of the tournament bell cut through the silence, marking the commencement of the battle. Both champions exuded a fluidity in their movements, a testament to their lifelong dedication to the mastery of their craft. Fiora's rapier danced and swirled through the air, a flickering sliver of deadly elegance. In contrast, Zed moved with the ethereal grace of a phantom, his shadowy shurikens slicing through the dense air with a lethal whirr that sent shivers down spines.

"Your skill is admirable," Zed conceded, a hint of respect bleeding into his otherwise cold and curt tone. Fiora's response was a cocky smirk, her emerald eyes glinting with determination, her grip on her rapier unwavering.

Their battle morphed into a deadly waltz, a mesmerizing blend of shadow and steel. Zed's conjured shadows clashed against Fiora's agile parries and swift lunges. The audience was caught in the throes of their deadly dance, every breath held, every cheer silenced by the palpable tension that thickened the air.

As Zed moved to deliver a decisive, potentially fatal strike, Fiora defied predictions. She twisted her body with unbelievable speed, her rapier deflecting Zed's shuriken with a dazzling display of skill before she lunged, her blade aiming straight for Zed's heart.

Zed, renowned for his swiftness, was not swift enough. His protective veil of shadows failed to fully shield him, and a sharp intake of breath betrayed his pain.

As the dust settled, the image that emerged was one of a victorious Fiora, standing tall and proud, and Zed, the Master of Shadows, kneeling on the ground nursing a wound on his arm. The crowd broke into a deafening roar, Fiora's name echoed from every corner of the arena. She responded with a dignified nod, basking in her well-deserved glory.

"An unexpected outcome, but a welcome one," Fiora declared, extending a hand to Zed. Despite his defeat, the Master of Shadows accepted her offer with a nod of respect.

However, Fiora's unexpected triumph over Zed disrupted the predicted course of the tournament. This unforeseen victory promised a shift in the dynamics of the tournament, an unpredictable turn of events that would undoubtedly keep everyone on the edge of their seats.

A Clash of Chaos and Strategy

In the tumultuous center of the tournament storm, Lux, the Lady of Luminosity, and Jinx, the Loose Cannon, were pitted against each other in the expansive arena. The contrast between the two champions was stark; Lux, a radiant emblem of hope and a master of strategic combat, faced Jinx, an embodiment of unpredictable chaos and frenzied havoc. As the spectators waited in anticipation, the referee gestured, his hand cutting through the air with authority to signal the commencement of the duel.

True to her reputation, Jinx sprang into action without any preamble. She hurtled towards Lux, her maniacal laughter echoing through the arena as she fired round after round from her arsenal. Yet, in the face of this onslaught, Lux maintained a cool, collected demeanor, her wand pulsating with a gentle but steady glow.

"Can't touch this, Jinx!" Lux taunted, effortlessly sidestepping a rocket aimed at her. Without missing a beat, she retorted with a swift incantation, luminous chains springing from her wand in an attempt to ensnare her erratic adversary.

Jinx responded with a triumphant cackle, "You'll have to be faster than that!" Displaying her unpredictable agility, she performed a cartwheel that took her out of Lux's spell's trajectory, causing the chains of light to explode harmlessly against the arena floor.

The spectators were entranced by the spectacle of the duel. Each meticulously planned move by Lux was met with a wildly unpredictable response from Jinx, pushing the boundary of traditional combat tactics.

In the throes of the unfolding chaos, Lux spotted a fleeting opportunity. As Jinx momentarily paused to reload her weaponry, Lux seized the moment to call upon her ultimate ability. "Final Spark!" she cried, and a brilliant beam of pure, concentrated light surged from her wand, engulfing the battlefield in a blinding illumination.

Jinx's reflexes were renowned, but this time, they failed her. The beam struck her squarely, propelling her backwards to crash onto the arena floor.

The crowd exploded into a cacophony of shock and cheers. Lux extended her hand to help Jinx, who, after a moment of bewildered surprise, accepted it with a hearty, appreciative laugh.

"Didn't see that one coming," Jinx conceded, brushing dust off her outfit. "Guess my chaos couldn't outshine your strategic light show this round."

While the encounter concluded with Lux's strategic mastery overpowering Jinx's chaotic unpredictability, the memorable clash between these contrasting styles added another captivating chapter to the unfolding narrative of the tournament.

The Final Duel

As the sun set over Runeterra, its fading rays cast an orchestra of shadows across the colossal coliseum, creating an eerily beautiful spectacle. The remaining gladiators, Lux and Zed, took measured steps into the arena. A blanket of silence fell over the audience, the anticipation so palpable it was almost a physical presence. Both champions had carved their path through formidable adversaries to reach this climactic confrontation, their trials and victories culminating in this singular moment.

"May the best champion win," Lux declared, her voice resonating in the silent stadium, the gravity of the impending duel lending her words a sober weight.

In response, Zed, the Master of Shadows, gave a silent nod, the setting sun casting an ominous gleam in his eyes. They were the serene epicenter of an approaching tempest, bracing themselves for the final battle. The tournament had been a whirlwind of shock, excitement, joy, and despair, all weaving into the intricate tapestry leading up to this grand finale.

The audience held their collective breath, hearts pounding in synchrony as the referee's arm rose. With a swift, decisive motion, he signaled the start of the tournament's final duel.

Lux wasted no time, igniting the battlefield with a dazzling array of her light magic, aiming to confine Zed within her radiant assault. But Zed, with his mastery over the elusive art of shadow manipulation, danced through Lux's attacks, moving as one with the encroaching twilight. Their distinct styles painted a mesmerizing tableau of opposition, a celestial dance of light and shadow battling for supremacy.

"You're not going easy on me, are you?" Lux teased, her voice light as she expertly deflected Zed's razor-edged shurikens with her prismatic barrier.

Zed remained silent, his only response was to intensify his onslaught, his shadow clones pressuring Lux into retreat. But Lux was as persistent as the sun she emulated. "Don't underestimate the light, Zed!" she warned, her energy concentrating into a powerful Luminous Singularity.

As the duel progressed, it became evident that this was not just a test of strength and skill. It was a clash of ideologies, a face-off between polar opposites, and above all, it was a testament to their unfaltering determination and resolve.

As the evening waned and the sun sank below the horizon, the battleground was lit by the soft glow of the stars, punctuated by the flashes of magic that sparked between the two adversaries. Under this ethereal illumination, Lux and Zed fought on, neither yielding nor faltering, their struggle echoing the intense uncertainty of the outcome. The spectators watched, utterly enraptured by the climactic battle unfolding before them, a fitting grand finale to a tournament that had been a rollercoaster of high drama and relentless tension.

In the Heat of Battle

The duel raged on. Underneath the starlit sky, the ground of the coliseum trembled beneath the intensity of Lux and Zed's battle. Their exchanges escalated from simple strikes and defenses to spectacular displays of magic, painting the night canvas with swirling lights and dancing shadows.

Lux was the first to seize the offensive, her staff glowing brighter than ever. "Light Binding!" she cried out, sending two ethereal chains of radiant energy towards Zed. The crowd gasped as the chains raced across the battlefield, the anticipation building up like a crescendo.

In response, Zed vanished, his form dissipating into shadows before reappearing a safe distance away, his evasion as seamless as the night itself. His shurikens whirred through the air, heading straight for Lux, who swiftly raised her Prismatic Barrier, her defensive spell ricocheting the blades away with a resounding clash.

"Your shadows can't hide you forever, Zed!" Lux taunted, her tone underlined with determination. Her staff was ablaze with light once more, and a blinding, concentric spiral of energy erupted from it.

Seeing this, Zed prepared himself, raising his arm as he channeled his shadow magic. As Lux's Final Spark came hurtling towards him, he split into multiple shadow clones, each dispersing in separate directions, causing her ultimate spell to blast harmlessly between them.

The spectators were on the edge of their seats, their cheers and gasps providing the soundtrack to the intense battle. The strategic brilliance of Lux and Zed's evasive shadow artistry combined to create a spectacle that would be etched in the annals of the tournament's history.

As the minutes slipped by, it became clear that neither champion was willing to concede. They fought tooth and nail, their spirits refusing to waver under the crushing weight of the stakes. Their battle was not just for victory in the tournament, but also for the honor and pride of the factions they represented. Amid the cheers, the spells, and the drama, one thing was certain – the grand finale of the tournament was turning out to be an epic clash that Runeterra would remember for ages to come.

An Unforeseen Turn

Despite the extraordinary clash of their abilities, the balance of the battle seemed to hang in equilibrium. Lux, with her radiant energy, and Zed, with his shadowy manipulation, were so evenly matched that no clear victor was in sight.

However, the tide of the battle began to turn when Lux took a calculated risk. With a defiant yell, she charged at Zed, her staff blazing with light. But Zed, anticipating this, smirked as he prepared his ultimate ability, "Death Mark." As Lux neared, he leaped into the air, his form dissolving into shadows, before appearing behind her.

Lux's eyes widened as she felt Zed's presence behind her, but it was too late. Zed's Death Mark was upon her, and she felt a sharp pain as his shadows tore into her. The crowd watched in shocked silence as Lux was thrown to the ground, her radiant magic flickering weakly.

Zed stood tall, his form surrounded by an aura of darkness. It seemed victory was within his grasp. But as he moved towards Lux, the crowd held their breath, waiting for Lux's response.

With a grunt of effort, Lux slowly rose to her feet, her staff flickering weakly. She looked at Zed, her eyes glowing with determination.

"Light is more resilient than you think, Zed," she said, her voice echoing throughout the silent stadium.

As Zed watched in surprise, Lux raised her staff high above her head. "Final Spark!" she yelled. A blinding, colossal beam of energy erupted from her staff, aimed directly at Zed.

A Radiant Victory

Zed reacted too late. The beam struck him square in the chest, sending him flying back. As the dust settled, Lux stood victorious, her light magic casting long, triumphant shadows in the coliseum.

The crowd erupted into deafening cheers. Lux, the Lady of Luminosity, had won the final duel. Despite the odds, her resilience and her unwavering faith in the power of light had seen her through.

As she helped Zed to his feet, the Master of Shadows nodded at her in respect. "Your light is indeed powerful, Lux," he said, his voice grudging, yet sincere.

As the cheers continued, Lux held her staff high, its light reflecting in the eyes of every spectator. The grand tournament was over, and Lux was the undisputed champion. But more than that, she had proven that even in the face of darkness, the light could always find a way to shine through.

Secrets of the Prize

The noise of the final duel between Lux and Zed echoed throughout the coliseum as Ashe and Zed, off to the sidelines, remained engrossed in their investigation. Armed with the information they had gathered thus far, they were on the cusp of uncovering the truth about the Tournament Master's mysterious prize.

Zed, focused on a worn-out parchment, muttered under his breath, "There's a pattern here, a sort of code, but I can't quite decipher it."

Ashe, holding a pendant that glowed with an eerie blue light, replied, "And this pendant, it has the same symbol as on the parchment. They're connected somehow."

Suddenly, a beam of light shot up from the pendant, illuminating the symbols on the parchment. The symbols began to shift and turn, as if being deciphered before their very eyes.

"The pendant! It's a key," exclaimed Zed, looking at the symbols now forming coherent phrases. Ashe read aloud the translated text, her voice steady, "The prize...it's the 'Heart of the Frejlord.' It's said to grant immense power to the bearer...power enough to reshape the world."

Both of them exchanged a glance, understanding the magnitude of what they had just discovered. This wasn't just a simple prize, it was a powerful artifact that could have disastrous implications if it fell into the wrong hands.

"We need to inform the others," Ashe said, urgency clear in her voice. But just as they turned to do so, a shadow loomed over them.

"Ah, I see you've discovered the truth," a voice echoed around them. It was the Tournament Master, his face hidden behind a hood, an perplexing smile playing on his lips.

As the chapter closed, Ashe and Zed stood facing the Tournament Master, their discovery about the prize leaving them with more questions than answers and a new, far more dangerous challenge ahead.

The Grand Finale

As the moon bathed the grand coliseum in its pale light, the grand finale of the tournament was about to commence. All eyes were on Zed and Lux, the remaining champions standing opposite each other, their figures casting long shadows on the battleground.

Zed, shrouded in mystery as always, concealed his emotions behind his mask, while Lux's face, illuminated by her staff, showed her determination. The air crackled with electricity, the tension tangible, as they waited for the starting signal.

The Tournament Master, perched high on his throne, raised his hand and declared, "May the final duel...commence!"

Zed was quick on the draw, shadows swirling around him as he sent a flurry of shurikens towards Lux. She reacted swiftly, a barrier of light materializing in front of her, reflecting Zed's attack.

The crowd cheered, equally divided in their support, as the two champions danced a deadly ballet, offense and defense interchanging swiftly.

Zed, relying on deception, created shadow clones, surrounding Lux from all sides. "Now, where will you go, lady of luminosity?" he taunted, his voice echoing from all directions.

Lux, however, stood her ground. "Light is but a single element, Zed, it is also warmth, guidance, and...hope," she declared. As she said this, she began to spin her staff rapidly, creating a whirlwind of light around her.

The blinding light made the shadow clones vanish, and before Zed could react, Lux focused her energy, her staff glowing brighter than ever, "Final Spark!"

A beam of light erupted from her staff, barreling towards Zed. But Zed, just a moment before impact, used his shadow to teleport away, appearing behind Lux. "Well played, Lux. But this isn't over."

As the chapter closed, the two champions stood ready to resume their duel, the crowd on the edge of their seats, the outcome of the grand finale still uncertain.

Victor's Spoils

Exhausted, Zed and Lux stood across from each other. After a strenuous duel, Lux emerged victorious. The arena was filled with cheers, chants, and applause from the crowd. Amidst the thunderous applause, the Tournament Master descended from his throne, his robe flowing around him.

"Ladies and Gentlemen of Runeterra," he began, silencing the crowd with his commanding voice. "We have our champion!"

He turned to face Lux, a wry smile playing on his lips. "Well fought, Lady of Luminosity. You've shown us the power of light today."

Lux, still catching her breath, nodded, a weary but triumphant smile on her face. "Thank you, Tournament Master. Your tournament brought out the best in all of us."

He gestured her forward, and from within his robe, he pulled out a small, intricate box, covered in ancient runes. Lux took it gingerly, her eyes wide with curiosity.

"As promised, the victor's spoils," he announced. "This box contains a relic of immense power, a token of the First Ascendant. Use it wisely."

Lux glanced at the crowd and then at Zed, who nodded at her. She turned the box in her hands and opened it. Inside was an amulet, glowing with a soft light. Lux gasped as the amulet pulsed with magical energy. It felt warm and strangely familiar, like a piece of a puzzle she didn't know she was missing.

"Remember, Lux," the Tournament Master added, his voice dropping to a whisper audible only to her, "the greatest power comes from within."

And with that, he stepped back, leaving Lux holding the amulet high above her head. The crowd erupted into cheers once more, their cries echoing into the night, and Lux stood victorious, wondering about the amulet's true power and the true identity of the Tournament Master.

As the cheers slowly died down and the crowd began to disperse, Lux, Ezreal, and Ashe exchanged glances, their minds already racing with new questions and possible adventures ahead. The Tournament may have ended, but their quest was far from over.

A New Path

As the dust settled on the grand coliseum, the champions found themselves in the quiet solitude of the aftermath. The revelries of the crowd had faded into distant echoes, leaving them with their thoughts.

In the now deserted stands, Zed found himself reflecting on his loss. He had entered the tournament with a thirst for victory, yet found that his defeat had humbled him. He had always relied on the shadows, but now, he wondered if he could learn something from Lux's light. He was a master of shadows, but there was a balance in all things, and perhaps it was time to acknowledge that.

Garen, having been bested by Fiora earlier, had his pride slightly wounded. However, he also felt an unexpected sense of relief. The tournament had freed him from the expectations of his kingdom, even if for a brief period. He found himself respecting Fiora more, not just as an opponent but as a true warrior.

Fiora, on the other hand, had a newfound respect for herself. She had faced tough opponents, including Garen, and each duel had honed her skills further. The tournament had been a testament to her determination and skill, reinforcing her belief in herself.

Ezreal and Lux, although having uncovered the identity of the Tournament Master, were left with a sense of incomplete understanding. The mystery of the prize gnawed at them, pushing them towards a new journey of discovery.

As for Ashe, she felt a sense of peace. She had not won the tournament, yet she had discovered something valuable - an inner strength she hadn't known existed. She had faced Zed, a formidable foe, and even though she lost the match, she did not feel defeated.

Jinx sat amidst the wreckage of her duels, a wide grin on her face. She had taken risks, played by her own rules, and had the time of her life. Victory or defeat did not matter to her, as long as she had her fun.

As the sun began to set, painting the sky in hues of orange and purple, each champion left the coliseum, taking a piece of the tournament with them. The battles had tested their spirits and will, leaving them with unforgettable memories and lessons.

They had begun the tournament as champions, warriors, rivals. But they ended it with the understanding that they were much more than that - they were seekers, survivors, and above all, they were the heart of Runeterra. They had learned, grown, and evolved. Each had found a new path, a new perspective, forever changing their approach towards the battles that lay ahead.

The Master Unveiled

The morning after the tournament, the champions were summoned back to the coliseum, the reason unclear. The echo of their footsteps filled the air as they entered the great stone arena, their faces etched with curiosity and wariness.

Standing in the middle of the arena was the Tournament Master, his usual robe replaced by a suit of shining armor. The sunlight glinted off his armor, making him appear as a figure from a tale of old.

"Champions of Runeterra," he began, his voice echoing around the stadium. "I owe you an explanation. For the true purpose of this tournament and for who I am."

Ezreal stepped forward, his brow furrowed. "So, you're finally going to tell us? You kept us in the dark throughout the tournament."

The Tournament Master removed his helmet, revealing a familiar face. "I believe it is time."

Gasps echoed through the arena as they saw the face of Jarvan IV, the crowned prince of Demacia, beneath the helmet. The champions stared, their expressions ranging from surprise to disbelief.

"Jarvan?" Garen exclaimed, his eyes wide. "You were the Tournament Master?"

Jarvan nodded. "Yes, I was. I had my reasons, Garen, for keeping my identity a secret."

"But why?" Ashe questioned, stepping forward. "Why host this tournament?"

Jarvan sighed, his gaze falling upon each champion. "I wanted to understand. Understand each of you, your strengths, your resolve, your spirit. The conflicts in Runeterra often overshadow these aspects."

"The tournament was a way to bring out the best in each of you," he continued. "To give you a platform where your talents could shine undimmed by political squabbles or personal rivalries. And to help you realize your potential, beyond the realms of your respective factions."

Ezreal crossed his arms. "That's a noble cause, but why the secrecy? Why didn't you just tell us?"

"Would you have seen me as just Jarvan, the Tournament Master, and not as the Prince of Demacia?" Jarvan asked. "Would you have fought with the same determination and freedom?"

There was a silence as the champions considered his words. They glanced at each other, the reality of his words sinking in.

"So, what now?" Jinx broke the silence, her gaze flicking between Jarvan and the others.

"Now," Jarvan began, a determined glint in his eyes, "we use what we've learned. Not as separate entities, but as united champions of Runeterra. To protect and serve our world, together."

As Jarvan's words echoed through the coliseum, the champions looked at each other, a newfound understanding in their eyes. They had begun their journey as individual champions, but now, they stood united, ready to face the future as one.

Aftermath

As the champions began to disperse, Jarvan IV returned to his palace in Demacia. The grandeur of the royal halls did little to lessen the weight of what had transpired. He ordered the guards to leave him alone in his chambers, and they obeyed without question, leaving him to his solitude.

The room was filled with silence, interrupted only by the clinking sound of his armor as he moved. Jarvan walked over to an ornate mirror hanging on the wall, its gilded edges reflecting the royal banners of Demacia.

But this mirror was no ordinary artifact. As Jarvan gazed into it, the mirror started to ripple like water disturbed by a pebble, its reflection distorting and changing. An image flickered into view, a chilling, dark vista, a stark contrast to the golden hues of the palace - the Void.

A voice emerged from the mirror, devoid of warmth or compassion. "Well done," it said, the voice resonating within the chamber's stone walls.

Jarvan stood still, his face betraying no emotion. He looked at his reflection in the mirror, his features overlaid with the swirling darkness of the Void. "We now know the strengths of the champions, but more importantly, we know all of their weaknesses," the voice continued.

Without a word, Jarvan reached for the amulet around his neck. It was identical to the one that had been given as the tournament prize - an artifact of unknown origins and power.

As he touched the amulet, his eyes glowed with an unnatural light. There was a disturbing tranquility in his expression, suggesting the prince was not entirely in control.

"Everything is going as planned," Jarvan responded, his voice sounding eerily detached, echoing the voice from the mirror.

A shadow crept over the palace, plunging the royal halls into darkness. Outside, the citizens of Demacia looked up to see a swirling vortex of darkness spreading across the sky.

The Void was stirring once again, its cycle beginning anew. And at its helm, under the influence of an ominous amulet, was Jarvan IV, the Prince of Demacia. This shocking revelation left the future of Runeterra teetering on a precarious edge, marking a foreboding end to the champions' tournament, and opening a new chapter of peril.

A Strange Disturbance

The grandeur of the tournament had faded, leaving the arena filled with echoes of the battles fought and victories won. Each champion, their spirits molded by their experiences, set off on their respective paths, forever marked by the contest's trials.

Ashe returned to the cold solitude of the Freljord, her ice-encrusted bow serving as a chilling reminder of the fierce duel she'd fought. Fiora headed back to her noble house in Demacia, the mark of the grand duel still visible on her rapier. Lux, her heart heavy with what she'd learned about the Tournament Master, took to her studies with renewed vigor, determined to unravel the mysteries she'd unearthed.

Thresh, his chains clinking in satisfaction, disappeared into the ethereal world, while Ezreal and Jinx embarked on new adventures, their shared experience in the tournament forging a unique bond between them. Garen returned to his knightly duties, the weight of his duel with Fiora still etched in his memory, while Zed melted back into the shadows of Ionia, contemplating the revelation of the Tournament Master's true identity.

As they journeyed on, each champion was struck by a strange disturbance. It was as if the very fabric of Runeterra itself was trembling, emanating a wave of energy that sent shivers down their spines. Then, a vision appeared before their eyes.

The future unfolded in a terrifying display. Cities crumbled under the might of monstrous creatures, the very essence of life seemed to drain from the land, and the champions themselves were locked in a desperate battle against an overwhelming force. It was a future filled with despair, with loss, with defeat.

They watched, frozen in shock, as they saw themselves fall one by one, their weapons clattering to the ground, their efforts futile against the might of the enemy. The vision ended as quickly as it had begun, leaving each champion breathless and filled with a newfound dread.

This was not a prophecy they had expected or wished for, but it was one they could not ignore. As the ominous image of the future lingered in their minds, each champion knew their journey was far from over.

Their paths had diverged, but their destinies remained intertwined. Armed with the knowledge they'd gained from the tournament and haunted by the vision of a doomed future, they would continue their journey, determined to defy fate and save Runeterra from the looming disaster.

Ripples of Consequences

In the depths of the grand palace, far from the eyes of Runeterran common folk, the Tournament Master, none other than King Jarvan IV himself, mulled over the events that had transpired.

The empty tournament grounds echoed with the remnants of the grand spectacle, a testament to the battles fought, victories won, and secrets revealed. Jarvan IV stood silently, gazing at the grand arena through the ornate window of his chambers.

The amulet around his neck hummed with power, a subtle reminder of the control it exerted over him. A dim reflection of the Void flickered in his eyes as he held the amulet, its aura pulsating in sync with his heartbeats.

A satisfied smile crept onto his lips. "Just as planned," he muttered, his voice barely audible, yet it resonated in the quiet room.

The champions, each formidable in their own right, had revealed not just their strengths but their vulnerabilities too. Their weaknesses were now laid bare for him to exploit, a prospect that filled him with dark anticipation.

His gaze shifted to the mirror once again, the image of the Void ever-present. A voice echoed from the depths of the otherworldly realm, acknowledging his report, "Well done."

He sighed, placing the amulet back beneath his royal garments. The tournament was over, but the game was just beginning.

"Every man has a beast within," he murmured, his eyes reflecting the disturbing vision each champion had seen. "And every beast can be tamed."

As the moonlight seeped into his chamber, illuminating the tournament master's face, the weight of his words hung heavy in the air. Each champion, their weaknesses now known, had a battle ahead, not just against the impending Void invasion, but against their inner demons as well.

Jarvan IV closed his eyes, a grim resolve etched on his face. The upcoming trials would test not only their mettle but the very essence of their spirit. The echoes of the past were still fresh, and the shadows of the future were growing longer.

But for now, the world of Runeterra was still, its champions unaware of the tumultuous journey ahead. Tomorrow would bring with it new mysteries, new battles, and a new struggle for survival.

The real tournament had just begun.

www.ingramcontent.com/pod-product-compliance
Lightning Source LLC
LaVergne TN
LVHW091729300125
802574LV00002B/205